Along Came a Dog

Some other books by Meindert DeJong:

BILLY AND THE UNHAPPY BULL
DIRK'S DOG BELLO
THE HOUSE OF SIXTY FATHERS
HURRY HOME, CANDY
THE LITTLE COW AND THE TURTLE
SHADRACH
SMOKE ABOVE THE LANE
THE TOWER BY THE SEA
THE WHEEL ON THE SCHOOL

Along Came a Dog

by **MEINDERT DeJONG**

Pictures by **MAURICE SENDAK**

HarperTrophy®

A Division of HarperCollinsPublishers

f DeJong

ALONG CAME A DOG
Text copyright © 1958 by Meindert DeJong
Text copyright renewed 1986 by Meindert DeJong
Illustrations copyright © 1958 by Maurice Sendak
Illustrations copyright renewed 1986 by Maurice Sendak

Library of Congress Catalog Card Number: 57-9265
ISBN 0-06-021421-X (lib. bdg.)
ISBN 0-06-440114-6 (pbk.)

For Hein Wessell, my friend,
as a sort of recompense of rewards,
for also having to be
my brother-in-law

CONTENTS

Along Came a Dog

CHAPTER I

The Man Who Talked to Animals

THE MAN was in the chicken coop. It was early on a Sunday morning in April. Daylight had not yet come to the farm, and the makeshift chicken coop up in the horse barn above the empty horse stables was dim and dark, and the chickens were still sleeping on the roost. But the man's stirring about in the darkness awakened the chickens. The whole row of white chickens

1

with the big rooster in their midst rose up on the roost pole, peered, nervous and unseeing, at the shadowy man.

Then a little red hen squeezed out of the long white row, hopped down from the roost pole to the front edge of the roost, and opened her wings as if to fly out to the man. She did not quite trust herself to make the plunge into the darkness over the floor. She weaved and teetered, a small rusty blob against the dim, chalky whiteness of the row of chickens behind her on the roost pole.

"Don't you do it," the man said to the bobbing little hen. "If you fly down, they'll all come down. And that's exactly why I got up way before dawn to clean this hen house—I didn't want any chickens underfoot."

The little hen gathered herself, peered eagerly toward the sound of his voice. "Not that, either!" the man warned her. "Don't you dare try to fly to my shoulder. It'll get them all started, and I've got to have more time with this floor. Golly, it's all ice! I didn't realize it could get cold enough in here to freeze ice under a foot of straw."

His eyes swept along the chickens on the roost. "Ice under straw! Gosh, if it got that cold in here, it'll be a wonder if some of you didn't freeze your combs or toes," he observed to himself. "No, stay there," he ordered the little red hen. "Just close those wings. And I'll close my mouth so you won't try to find me by the sound of my voice."

He began scraping at the ice with a spade. But as he stooped to reach under the roost to scrape at a stubborn patch of ice there, the little hen stepped off the roost and on to his stooped back. The man jerked erect. The little hen ran up his back and balanced herself on his shoulder.

"Oh, you! You would think of that! Well, if that's where you've got to be, then hang on. I'm going to get all this ice and dirty straw off the floor and shoveled out the window before the rest of them come down."

The little red hen shifted on the man's shoulder, came close to his cheek, excited by the sound of his voice.

"You'd be even more excited if you knew it was spring outside," the man told her. "It's hard to believe in here—it's all winter and ice in this coop, but spring came in the night. Honest!"

The little hen started nibbling his cheek, but

the man began scraping at the stubborn ice again.
The little hen clung fiercely to his shoulder, balancing herself the best she could. At last the man
finished scraping the ice and shoved it to the
dirty bedding straw that he had piled before a
window. "Now come and see," he told the little
hen. He clambered over the straw pile and pried
the window out of its casing, set it against the
wall. Slowly, to give the little hen time to change
her position, he leaned far out of the window

opening. "See? Spring! It came in the night. Feel it all soft and warm and wonderful? And it's here to stay."

The little hen on his shoulder outside the window stood absolutely still, and the soft spring warmth that had come to the land in the night came welling up to her from the ground far below. She flapped her wings.

The man laughed softly. "If you could crow, now you would crow, wouldn't you? Hey! Let's let them all know it's spring. Let winter out of the coop and spring in. Yeah, that's what I'll do—take all the windows out, and let this whole first wonderful day of spring come into the coop."

It had taken hours, but now the floor of the hen house was dry and clean, fanned to dryness by the breezes that came warmly through the row of open windows. And now the man came with crisp, clean, new straw. He dumped it in scattered mounds over the floor, and immediately the waiting flock attacked the mounds. The hen house rustled with the crispness of new straw.

And the sun came out! Sunlight suddenly glistened on the gleaming straw. The whole hen house became still busier. The flock turned the straw and spread the straw. Straw sprayed and straw flew. The little red hen was right in the midst of the digging, kicking, scratching white flock, digging herself a hole, almost burying herself in straw. Only the rooster stood idle amid his hard-working flock.

But the sun was out, the sun was rising in the sky. Importantly the rooster strode across the floor, hopped up to a window sill, filled his chest, and crowed a mighty crow—to crow the sun up in the sky and sunlight into his busy hen house.

The little hen poked her head up from the hole she had dug and looked at the crowing rooster. She thoughtfully looked from the rooster in the window sill to the high row of nests that rose against the end wall of the hen house. She started to dig again, but then she hurried through the loose straw to the nests. The time had come to lay an egg.

Ignoring the rustling busyness all about her, and the glory of sunshine that the rooster had crowed into the yellow straw, the little hen flew up to the highest perch before the top row of nests. The time had come to lay an egg. It was a proud thing to lay an egg—a proud and important thing. But after the endless cold winter it was so long since the little hen had laid an egg that she had all but forgotten which one of the nests in the top row of nests was her favorite. She nervously ran back and forth on the high perch, trying to remember where she must lay her first egg of spring.

Suddenly the little hen remembered. It was the last nest in the row. She scurried to the end of the perch, hustled into the nest. She fussed with the straw in the nest, picked up single straws and laid them beside her just so. She felt something hard and cold under her, tried to wriggle it out of her way, but then she remembered—it was her nest egg. With her bill she tenderly hooked a tiny frosted light bulb from under the straw, tenderly tucked it under her. It was cold and dusty, and it had a brass socket, but the little hen loved her nest egg, loved to lay her brown egg beside the little white light bulb, for then it almost seemed as if she'd laid two eggs.

The little hen was all settled, the light bulb was beginning to get warm under her, she sat quietly looking out over the busy hen house—but there came the man! Instinctively the little hen ducked deep down in the nest, because laying an egg was now—and for all time—an important, secret, private thing. But she secretly watched the man. Suddenly she sat bolt upright.

The man was prying at a little slide door in the wall just above the floor. Now he pulled the slide way up, and there it was—the square opening in the wall. And the little hen remembered across the long winter that from that opening a ramp led down from the high hen house to the barnyard below. It spelled freedom to the little hen —freedom in spring. Freedom to go up and down the long ramp, freedom to roam. A great excitement stirred in the little hen.

A great excitement stirred down below among the whole white flock. White hens eagerly crowded around the man and the new opening he had made in the wall. White heads and necks poked toward the opening, but pulled back again. None of the chickens seemed to dare to be the first to go down the long ramp to freedom. They clustered around the opening, nervous and uncertain. The big rooster stayed well behind the huddle of nervous hens.

8

At that exciting moment the little hen's egg
came. She hastily fluttered from the nest to the
perch; but then, in spite of her eagerness to get to
the opening in the wall, she had to cackle out the
proud news of her egg—her first egg of spring.

She ran wildly along the perch cackling and
shouting her announcement to the hen house
below. The rooster on the floor began hoarsely

9

cackling along with her. The huddled chickens
for the moment forgot the opening in the wall,
started cackling in chorus along with the rooster.
The little hen cackled back. The man clapped
his hands to his ears. "Quiet!" he yelled above
the shrillness. "Please, a little quiet. One egg
has been laid, and you all act as if she'd laid a
crateful." He walked over to the nests and the
cackling, pacing little hen. "So you laid an egg,
and you're proud. Well, I'm proud of you, too.
But still it's only one little brown egg—you didn't
lay a dozen, and you didn't lay that light bulb—
so shall we calm down? Anyway, I've got things
for you to do. All these high-strung white hens—
they want to go down the ramp, they're crazy to
go outdoors, but they don't dare. And that
rooster's just as scared of the newness and bigness
outside. So shall you and I show them the way
down the ramp?"

He carried the little hen to the opening, got
down on hands and knees, reached out as far as
he could, and set her down on one of the crosspieces nailed on top of the ramp to give the
chickens a toehold for climbing up and down the

steep slant of the ramp. But the little hen suddenly had difficulty getting her toes to clutch the thick crosspiece on which he had set her. She flapped her wings, and tipped and teetered. "Now don't you get nervous and jittery and excited like the others," the man at the opening scolded her. He once more placed her squarely on the crosspiece, waited for her to clamp her toes around it, then withdrew his hand.

The little hen stood alone on the high ramp. She peered timidly at the ground far below her. Her toehold suddenly shifted. She cocked her head, stared desperately at her toes. She lifted one foot, trying for a better hold, tried to dig her nails into the soft wood of the crosspiece. They wouldn't take hold. Suddenly, with a queer, choked-off squawk, she tipped forward, and tumbled down the long slant of the ramp. She wildly beat her wings to slow her fall, but she fluttered and stumbled and slid all the way down the ramp. She managed to land upright, but she landed in the middle of a mud puddle at the foot of the ramp. She stood absolutely still, peering down at her feet in the mud.

At the top of the ramp, the man scrambled up off his knees, and hurried down the stairs to get to the little hen.

But now that the little red hen had gone down the ramp in whatever clumsy, frantic manner, the first white hen got courage also to go down the ramp. Behind her the rooster and the whole flock came streaming, but they went no farther than the little hen. They crowded around her in the mud puddle. Wary and unsure and nervous, the rooster and all the flock kept their eyes away from the bigness and brightness around them, stayed in a huddle, stupidly staring at the little hen in their midst.

The man came to stand behind the crowded flock. He leaned over the white chickens. "Don't tell me your first step into freedom you got your toes stuck in the mud," he joked with the little red hen. He stooped and reached out to pull her out of the mud. But as he stooped over them, the whole nervous, huddled flock exploded up around him in a thunder of wings, scattered wildly in all directions, scuttled away over the barnyard. The man stared at it in startled surprise. Only the little hen remained in the mud puddle.

"Why, all I did—I just stooped over them," the amazed man said to the little hen. He stooped once more to pick her up. Something big, black slid under him. The man snatched up the little hen, jerked erect, gaped at a big black dog that came creeping, almost swimming through the mud puddle. The dog pushed his head between the man's feet, lay trembling and silent.

The man stepped back from the dog. "So *you're* what scared them. They saw you coming. But where did you come from so suddenly?"

The dog squeezed himself ahead, crawled between the man's feet in the same swimming crawl. The perplexed man looked from the dog to the little red hen he was holding. "Well, what do you want of me?" he started to say to the dog. Suddenly he jerked his eyes back to the little hen. The little hen had no toes! All her toes were gone! In sorrowful silence the man looked at the little hen's toeless feet.

"I was afraid it would happen—all that ice under a foot of straw," he said at last. "One of those cold nights of winter you froze your toes, didn't you? And now they just came off. . . . But it didn't hurt," he sort of comforted himself and the little hen. "These past weeks they just turned to wood, didn't they? And now they came off in the mud, but you didn't feel a thing, did you? It didn't hurt."

The little hen twisted in the man's arms, looked perkily up at his talking lips, tried to nibble them. "No," the man said, "it didn't hurt."

At the sound of the man's soft words as he talked to the little red hen, words on words, the dog wriggled between the man's feet, trying to dare to wag his tail, trying to dare to look up at the man. His tail quivered, but he couldn't quite look up.

The dog's humble actions made the man aware of him again. "Look at him," he said to the little hen. "He acts as if there isn't a bone in his body or a brain in his head. You'd think he was jelly. But just from hearing me talk to you, he's put one idea in that brain of his. He figures I'm a pushover, and that I'm going to give him a home here."

He bent down to the dog. "That's what you thought or hoped, didn't you? Just because of all my talk. How could you know that I've got this crazy habit of talking to animals? But you can stop hoping. You can't stay here."

He turned to the little hen. "No toes, just bare knucklebones—now how are you going to manage?" He stood and thought. "Golly, what a time you picked to come," he told the dog. "What a hopelessly poor time."

"Isn't it queer, though," he said half to himself and the little hen, "for him to come just at the exact moment your toes came off? And just after you'd laid your first egg of spring. Why, it was like that, too, last year, when that pack of dogs came. You were laying your first egg then, too. You'd stolen away somewhere in a clump of weeds to lay your first egg, and so you escaped the slaughter—the only one those dogs didn't destroy. One little red hen left from a whole red flock. And now with no toes there isn't much left of you, is there?"

He impatiently turned to the dog. "And now *you* come along! Oh, I know you had nothing to do with this—she froze her toes weeks ago—but isn't it queer, you coming along just at that moment?" He stood for a while as if going over the odd idea that had jumped into his head. It seemed to make up his mind. "Up!" he said to the dog. "I may be a pushover, but not for dogs—not after what they did to that red flock—and I'm right now taking you for a long ride to get you as far away from here as I can. Come along!"

He turned away and with the little red hen on his arm strode out of the barnyard and toward an old car parked in the drive beside the house. Behind him the dog obediently got up, dragged himself on weak, hopeless legs after the man. The man got in the car, then first noticed he still held the little hen. "Hey, forgot about you in all my fretting over that dog. Maybe it's just as well you come along. With all your toes gone you're now so different I don't know what the rest of the flock might do to you. This way you'll be safe from them while I decide what I have to do with you."

He placed the little hen on the seat between his legs, opened the door on the other side of the car, patted the seat.

In timid misery the big dog crawled up to the seat, flowed up to the seat as if there weren't a bone in his body. The man slammed the door shut, and started the car.

The dog, trying to make himself small and flat

on the seat beside the man, almost put his chin on the man's leg. He nervously jerked his head back. The car started down the driveway. The little red hen perked her head up, inquisitively looked over the rounding of the man's leg at the dog. The dog lifted his hopeless eyes to the little hen. His eyes stayed fixed on the little hen.

CHAPTER II

The Moon in the Barn

THE MAN and the little red hen were back from the ride. The man stood beside the car and looked at the little hen in a troubled way. From under the steering wheel the little hen peered up at him.

"Well, it's done," the man said. "We did it. We took him for a ride." He half-turned and looked back across the field as if expecting to see the big dog come trudging along the road. "It's bothering me," he told the little hen. "But what's

18

the good of my talking about it now? It's done. I guess you're the big problem now."

He lifted the little hen off the seat. "Nothing but knucklebones left," he observed somberly. "And what's the good of them? You certainly can't be in the high coop with the flock now— you couldn't get up and down the ramp. But even if you could, I'm afraid losing your toes has made you so different that they'll peck and maul you to death."

He uttered a short laugh. "There's really only one quick businesslike way to solve this problem. Chop off your head, and have you for dinner." He mockingly felt of the little hen's ribs. "Not very meaty, are you? Not much dinner." At a sound behind him he turned and threw a troubled look toward the road.

A big car was turning up the driveway. It drew up behind the old car. "The boss," the man said briefly to the little red hen. He straightened up.

A gray-haired man leaned out of the car. "Joe," he called, "troubles on my place. My prize mare is suddenly ready to have her first colt and she's having a terrible time. It's your Sunday off, but I've got to have you there. She's so scared, she's kicking her stall to slivers. She'll hurt herself. Maybe you can quiet her."

"I'll be right over," Joe said. "Just got to take care of this little hen a moment."

"What's wrong with her?"

"No toes," Joe said. "The old coop I rigged up over the horse stables isn't much good and she must have frozen her toes awhile back, and now they just dropped off. It sure is a problem what to do with her."

"Joe," the boss grunted, "chop her head off and eat her for dinner. You can't mess around with a toeless chicken."

"Yeah," Joe said tonelessly. "That's almost word for word what I was telling myself as you drove up. But this little hen—well, she's sort of a pet, guess I'm sort of sentimental about her. She's the only one left from the red flock that those dogs mauled."

"Joe, you know with frozen toes she'll most likely never lay another egg. Get it over with! Chop her head off, and then hustle over. Anything I do just seems to make that mare more nervous." He backed down the driveway.

"She laid an egg just before—" Joe started to say, then noticed that the car was driving away. "Get it over with," he muttered to himself. "Well, not today!" he suddenly decided out loud. He hurried across the yard, grabbed an old potato crate, carried it near the kitchen door, and pushed the little hen under the upside-down crate. The moment she was under the crate the little hen began scrambling and poking to get out. The man watched her. "I know it's a prison, but take my word for it, it's not a life sentence. This is just to keep you safe from the flock until I get back from the mare."

He stood as if he couldn't quite decide to go, couldn't quite make up his mind. "Got to go now. Got to help bring a homely, gawky colt into the world. All wonderful and all legs, and all helpless with those long legs. And you not enough legs—at least too short without your feet. But I'll be back. And then we're going to solve your problem, too. Somehow we'll solve it."

Suddenly relieved, and fully decided, he sprinted to the car.

Under the crate the little hen stood perfectly

still listening to the car rattling away down the road. Then, as if quite unaware that she had no toes, she began scurrying back and forth under the crate. She rapped and poked at the slats. She rasped her comb raw as she tried again and again to twist and screw her head through the narrow spaces between the slats.

From the barnyard came the busy, excited sounds of the flock, and the little hen suddenly caught sight of the steady procession of chickens going up and down the ramp and in and out of the high chicken coop, tasting and testing the new freedom. For a moment the little hen stood still. Then she began still more desperately scurrying back and forth. If it didn't bring her freedom, the meaningless, unhappy rushing under the crate was giving the little hen practice. She raced back and forth as if she'd run on knucklebones all her life. She hardly stumbled.

A butterfly settled on top of the potato crate. The little hen stopped, aimed a greedy eye, jumped for the butterfly. She crashed against a top slat of the crate. The slat was loose. It yielded. Its loose end poked up from the crate. The little hen leaped up again, hooked her bill over the top edge of the crate. Hanging by her bill, she flailed her wings against the slat, forced it up still more. She fell back exhausted, but when she saw the opening above her, she immediately jumped up and tumbled over the edge of the crate. The little hen was free. And there was the butterfly still flitting over the yard. The little hen immediately gave chase. The butterfly fluttered down to the barnyard with the little hen joyously pounding after it at the queer gait her shortened toeless legs had given her. She seemed to roll over the ground on her little round knucklebones.

At the edge of the barnyard seven white hens joined the little red hen, pelted with her after the butterfly. The rooster came running. He immediately had to make the chase important by calling to all the flock. Hens came racing from everywhere. Now the whole flock streamed after the little hen, changed directions with her whenever the butterfly shifted in its aimless flight. The big rooster pounded along in the midst of his hens.

Suddenly a breeze wafted the butterfly up and over the roof of the big hay barn that rose across the barnyard from the horse barn with the hen house. All at once the quarry was gone. The chase stopped dead in the middle of the barnyard. The flock stood foolishly looking at each other. But the rooster suddenly became enraged with the little red hen who had led them on this foolish chase.

In two strides he was at her. He rapped her head with slashing hammer blows of his hard bill. The blows struck the little hen's comb, rasped raw from rubbing against the slats of the potato crate. Her temper flared. She leaped up at the rooster, tried to rake and slash his chest. Her round knucklebones wouldn't rake, didn't slash, but one of the white hens noticed her strange, toeless feet. The hen darted under the rooster's chest, pecked a curious, investigating peck at one of the little hen's knucklebones.

With that one peck what had been a foolish springtime chase of a butterfly turned into something ugly. Other hens darted in. They struck the little hen down. In a moment she lay kicking and sprawling, but each hen still got in a blow and a peck. Desperately the little hen righted herself. In sheer strength of terror she squirmed and forced a path through the surrounding flock. The ugly, senseless blows still hammered down on her. At last she squeezed from under the pack, and, free from the flock, ran for her life across the empty barnyard.

For the moment the flock did not follow. For the moment there was only the small sound of the little hen's knucklebones on the hard-packed ground. The flock stood absolutely still, watching the queer run of the little red hen. Eyes gleamed, dark, excited eyes flickered. The queer run they were watching enraged and offended the flock. They came on. They overtook the little hen, surrounded her. Suddenly there was no more flight and no more fight in the little red hen. She flattened herself in their midst, bowed her neck, resigned herself to her end.

Wheezing hard, the big rooster now stepped in, angrily made a clearing for himself in the midst of the packed flock. Chugging throatily, dragging and scraping one wing on the ground, he made a circle path for himself around the little hen.

The flock had to wait for him. Their eyes flicked wickedly from the strutting rooster to the cowering little hen, but they stood back as once more the rooster chugged himself in an important circle around the little hen. At last he stepped before the little hen, stood over her. The flock came crowding in—the moment for the kill had come.

But the rooster's circling and important fussing had given the little hen a bit of breath, a mite of rest. A last rebellion flicked up in her. She fluttered up, tried to beat herself up into the air above the rooster and the crowding flock, fly over them. She couldn't.

The little hen had been knocked down into

the barnyard dirt so often, her feathers and wings were full of sand. As she tried to flutter up her beating wings threw dirt into the rooster's face, blinded him, befuddled him. Mad from the stinging sand in his eyes, eyes shut tight against the pain, the rooster struck out wildly in all directions. The flock scattered. The hens scuttled out of his reach.

In the confusion the little red hen ran across the barnyard as hard as she could run. The opening of the wide doorway to the basement of the big hay barn loomed dark before her. With all the strength left in her beaten little body she ran into the barn, hid in a back corner of the dark, shadowy barn.

The rooster, left all alone in the middle of the barnyard, shook and shook his head to clear his stinging eyes. His eyes cleared just in time for him to see the little hen scamper through the doorway into the basement of the barn. There went his enemy who had humiliated him before the whole flock. Forgetting the pain in his eyes, the rooster took after her. He called and commanded his flock to come. All the hens came. They streamed after him through the wide doorway.

In the darkness against the back wall of the basement the little red hen saw them come out of the sunlit yard. She panicked. She flew up, hit against something in the gloom of the crowded basement. It knocked her down. But as she fell back she landed on the thin edge of an empty bushel basket. She beat her wings, desperately tried to cling to the thin edge of the basket. The basket rocked, toppled, flipped over, and fell on top of her.

The little hen disappeared so suddenly, so completely, that the flock stopped in confusion in the middle of the shadowy barn. Then, near the doorway, there was a hen quarrel. The rooster, recalled to his duties, strode over to the fighting hens, stepped between them, and chased them out of the barn. He marched importantly after them, marched himself out of the barn. The whole white flock obediently streamed after him out of the barn. The little red hen had been forgotten as suddenly and completely as had been the butterfly.

Under the basket the bruised, exhausted little hen sat huddled and quiet. In the dimness under · the basket her head began to nod, and then she slept fitfully. She awoke with a start, slept again. When she once more woke up, it was completely dark under the basket. Dark night silence lay over the whole basement of the barn.

Then in the dark barn there was suddenly the stealthy, scratchy noise of a rat. The scratching went on. Other rats came. The night deepened, the rats became bolder, noisier. The basket suddenly jiggled on its handles as a rat leaped up on it to nibble and chisel away at an ear of dried corn it had found. Another rat came, tried to steal the corn. There was a battle above the little hen, the basket rocked wildly on its handles. A rat shrieked. The next moment all the rats suddenly rustled away and the barn lay completely silent.

After the rats were gone there was a big noise outside. Then light ranged and swept through the wide doorway, slid toward the overturned basket. Under the basket the little hen rose up in alarm, but then she recognized the sounds as the old rattletrap car came thumping up the driveway. Once more the lights of the car swept across the floor, almost reached the basket, but flicked out. The big darkness fell back into place.

Later a small light came, a moving, flickering light—a lantern. It went back and forth in the barnyard beyond the wide doorway, and the little red hen listened excitedly to the man's slow footsteps going back and forth in the barnyard. But the man did not come into the barn, did not come to her basket. By the light of his guttering lantern the man was reading the signs in the barnyard. He stooped, picked up a red tail feather. Grim faced, he straightened and looked up at the dark hen house. "Well, I knew I'd find just this the moment I saw that loose slat sticking up from the potato crate," he said harsh and loud up to the high coop. "You mauled her to death, and some dog or swamp animal came along and carried her away. Once she got out of that crate, she never had a chance."

The little hen peered from under the basket at the small spot of light from the lantern, listened excitedly to the man's loud, lone talking. The man suddenly strode past the wide doorway, his lantern swinging angrily.

Through the doorway patches of light from the swinging lantern rayed out for a moment as far as the bushel basket. By that brief bit of light the little red hen lunged from under the basket. The basket's sharp edge scraped her sore, torn comb as she struggled from under it, but she hardly noticed it. She ran after the man.

Outdoors, the old lantern suddenly guttered out. "Hanged if I don't get me a flashlight," the man barked irritably.

The light was gone, and the man was gone in the darkness. Like all chickens, the little hen could see utterly nothing in the dark. Helpless in the dark, the little red hen had to sink down where she was in the middle of the barn, had to listen helplessly to the man going away to the house.

Later, much later, the moon came out, moonlight slipped into the barn. For a brief moment cool, dim light flitted across the open doorway, then was gone as the moon slid behind a mass of clouds. In that momentary flit of moonlight the little hen saw something big, dark, silhouetted in the wide-open doorway. The little hen sat still as death.

It took long frozen moments for the black clouds to pass over the moon, then moonlight stood cool and grave in the doorway again. And in the moonlight in the doorway stood the dog. Across the barn the little hen and the big black dog looked at each other. Then the dog's bushy tail swung in such enormous friendliness—his wagging tail shook his body. With a sharp little cackle the little hen ran to the dog.

CHAPTER III

Duck Feet

THE LITTLE HEN followed the dog through the moonlit barnyard. The dog seemed to know exactly where he wanted to be. He led her straight to the kitchen door of the house.

At the house, the little hen, obeying her deep instincts, left the dog to hide under the broad leaves of a huge burdock plant growing beside the kitchen door. The dog threw himself full length before the kitchen door. The moon sank away into endless banks of clouds. The night went pitch dark. The night stayed dark.

The weasel came in a dark, flowing motion

33

out of the dark. In silence it went straight toward the slight dried blood smell still clinging to the little hen. Suddenly the weasel was at the burdock plant. There was no time for the dog to rise and leap. A growl pushed out of his throat. Like dark lightning the weasel vanished—a darkness gone into the darkness, as if the weasel had never been.

After the alarm of the weasel the dog lay alert, head on paws, eyes staring. As his eyes became accustomed to the darkness he patiently watched two skunks, each one going his exact slow way down the ruts in the driveway. The dog did not find it necessary to warn the skunks—they were far enough away from the little hen under the burdock plant.

He had become a different dog in the night. Not meek now, not beaten, spineless, but a dog with a firm purpose and a duty that he had put on himself—to guard and protect the little red hen.

Disturbance came again toward morning. A strange dog came carelessly snuffling along the big hay barn, padded across the yard toward the house, suddenly turned toward the burdock plant. In one leap from his lying position the big black dog hurtled himself before the burdock plant, threw himself about to face the intruder. He stood backed into the burdock, lips rolling, teeth savage. Short, stiff growls stuttered out of his throat.

The intruder dog started answering the growls, thought better of it, turned, and stalked away on stiff legs to show that he was not afraid—just not interested. But once out of sight behind the old car, he hustled himself down the drive and disappeared in the night.

The big dog started back to the kitchen door. There was a slight sound. Still angry and defiant, the dog began a growl. The kitchen door flung open. It was the man! Before the man the dog collapsed, lay guilty and meek and silent.

The man stepped out of the doorway into the dark yard. "So you found your way back—you're smarter than I thought," he said softly in the darkness. "But your timing is still bad. Of all nights to wake me up! First I'm up half the night with that mare and her new colt. Then when I come home around midnight I find the little hen murdered. And now when I'm trying to catch

a few hours of sleep—there you are again. Well, is there any reason I shouldn't make a bad night complete by taking you for still another ride? It's dark—this time it won't be so easy for you to follow the car and find your way back here—at least not from where I'm going to take you. Come along!"

All the night bravery was drained from the dog. Obedient to the man's order, he rose weak-kneed, dragged on behind the man to the car, and flowed in his boneless flow up to the seat. In meek silence he fitted himself into place on the seat.

In the driveway the headlights flared. Seeing the light, the little hen started to come from under the burdock plant. But the car rattled down the drive, the light went away. And blind in the dark, the little hen sank down under the leaves of the burdock plant.

The man had come back alone. And now it was between nine and ten o'clock—the middle of this sunny Monday morning—and the man was still around. He seemed to be back to stay, and he did a strange thing. He carried a rocking chair and a mail-order catalog from the house, and set the chair down on the packed ground in the middle of the deep barnyard. He sat down in the chair. He took the catalog from under his arm and placed it on his lap. Then he reached down, picked up the little red hen who had followed him, and set her on the catalog. He rocked himself a few lazy moments, looked at the little hen, and shook his head in amazement. "Here I thought you'd been murdered last night, and here I come back from taking that dog away, and there you are—beat up a bit, but full of life, and all in one piece!"

He fell silent, sat contentedly rocking and looking out over the barnyard. The white flock was busy. Hens were streaming up and down the long ramp. From out of the high-loft hen house sang the proud cacklings of many hens laying eggs. The man suddenly laughed. "I want to announce," he said slowly and importantly, "a holiday has been declared—a Sunday-on-a-Monday holiday. Mind you, and please let us be impressed—two Sundays in a row for me—it's an untold, unheard-of luxury. A holiday has been declared for me by the boss on the big farm."

He suddenly guffawed. "I took that dog for such a long ride," he told the little hen, "I almost got lost myself. Then on the way back, as I passed the big farm, I suddenly decided I might as well have a look at the mare. And there I walk into the barn, and there are the boss and his wife admiring the new colt. And they're so impressed with me and what I did for that mare, the boss tells me I've earned a whole free day.

"Of course I didn't tell him I was there because

of the dog. He'd think it silly—taking a stray dog for a ride instead of just shooting him. And if I'd told him—I know how the boss's mind works—it would have immediately made him think of you. Then if I'd had to tell him that I'd kept you instead of chopping your head off—well, I'd hate to think what he would have said. But I'm sure he would have been so disgusted, he'd never have given me a whole day off."

The man looked in lazy fondness at the little hen. The little hen lifted one foot and nibbled gently all the way around the smooth, bare knucklebone. "You feel just as lazy and beat up as I do," the man observed. Suddenly he threw himself around in the chair, sat staring. "Golly," he said slowly, "if that wasn't as if I saw something big and black just as it was sneaking around the hay barn. Naw, it couldn't be—I took him by such crazy twists and circles. It's just my silly conscience. That dog somehow manages to make me feel mean all over—he's so meek. If he'd only give me a dirty look when I finally shove him out of the car. But he gets out when I tell him, and there he stands on the road. It'll make me feel guilty all day."

He shook off the mood, looked at the little hen standing on the catalog in his lap. "Now for the experiment," he told her. "That's why I'm here in the barnyard in a rocking chair. I want you to get among the flock. It's safe—I promise. Today I'm your guarding rooster, and if one of the flock so much as makes a pass at you—" He set the little hen on the ground, pushed at her with his foot. "Come on, get going on your knucklebones. I want to see what they'll do to you for being without toes."

The little hen set off, wandered toward the foot of the ramp. At that moment the big rooster came out of the hen house, strutted down the ramp. Behind him, meek and admiring, seven hens followed him down the ramp. But the rooster saw the little red hen and stopped. All seven wives stopped behind him. The little hen was pecking at something at the foot of the ramp. She was quite unaware of the rooster above her. But the man in the rocking chair slid to the edge of the seat, slid the chair on its runners silently over the packed ground closer to the ramp, sat ready.

The rooster cleared the last four feet of the ramp and landed with a thud right beside the startled little hen. The seven white hens ran down the ramp. The little red hen looked up at the towering rooster, then timidly, meekly, properly, she squatted down in the dust before her lord and master. The rooster chugged angry noises at her. He dropped a threatening wing. Wing scraping the ground with a harsh, threatening sound, he twirled around the little hen. But his eye caught the gleam of a yellow kernel of corn stuck under the ramp. He immediately forgot his threats, seized the corn kernel and pushed it toward the little red hen. He proudly tapped the ground and clucked to all his flock to let them know about his great find. But he presented the kernel to the little hen.

Out of her crouch the little hen meekly reached for the kernel of corn. But one of the seven hens darted in, stole the kernel from under the little hen's beak. Furious, the little hen leaped up at the thief to force her to drop the kernel.

The man in the chair grabbed up the catalog, ready to hurl it. But the rooster, with fine impartiality, stepped between the two fighting hens, and, like any referee, neatly separated them. Impartially he gave both battlers a stern rap with his bill. Then, taking possession of the kernel of corn, and clucking with motherly softness, he presented the prized kernel—not to the little hen—but to the thieving white hen.

The disappointed little hen stood stock-still watching the white hen gobble the corn, then turned and ran to the man in the rocking chair as if to make a complaint.

The man sat chuckling. "No. No complaints. You haven't got a leg to stand on. The rooster's rooster brain is really working this morning. He accepted you as part of his flock—knucklebones or no knucklebones. He presented you with a prize morsel, and he punished you for fighting in the exact same way he punished his favorite white hen. And from now on, knucklebones or no knucklebones, my guess is, he'll protect you from the rest of the flock. But of course I can't help it that you're his number one hundred wife, and that the white hen was wife number one. That's the way of the world and the hen yard."

He looked fondly down at the little red hen. "Now keep moving among the flock. I want to see if the rest of the flock will accept you as one of them the way the rooster did. Then I'll know you're safe. I can't keep you under a potato crate the rest of your life."

The little hen wandered off. The man began looking through the mail-order catalog. Suddenly he stopped at a page, stared at it. "Flippers!" he told himself in some amazement. "Rubber flippers to strap to your feet to help you swim better . . . They would give you a powerful stroke . . ."

He looked up, stared thoughtfully at the little hen. "Naw, it's silly," he told himself. "You can't put duck feet on a chicken!"

But he got up and, thumb between the pages of the catalog, he walked over to the wide doorway of the basement of the barn. He stood in the doorway, surveying the jumble of old farm machinery and the clutter of baskets and boxes and farm tools that had been stored, stuffed, and crowded into the barn basement and hadn't been stirred for years. Then he saw what he wanted, wound his way among the cumbersome machinery to the back wall of the basement, and pulled down a rubber strap hanging there.

Eyes on his find, mind on his plans, he made his way back to the rocking chair, fished a jackknife out of his pocket, and began whittling and shaping the rubber strap. Once he slid from the chair, and with his thumb held on the blade of the knife, carefully measured the round impression the little hen's knucklebone foot had made in a ridge of loose dirt. He chuckled to himself and began gouging a round socket hole into the heel part of a tiny flipper he had shaped. He scraped and smoothed.

At last he held up two tiny rubber flippers, studied them critically, then went in search of the little red hen.

He found her in the middle of a mud puddle, trying to scratch for worms with her round, smooth knucklebones. He scooped her up. "Disgusted, aren't you? Getting exactly nowhere. Well, look—I made feet for you. Rubber feet! I don't expect you'll be able to dig for worms with them, but if you could only get up and down the ramp with them—well, then you could stay with the flock."

He forced the sockets of the rubber flippers over the knucklebones. "They've got to be tight, or you can't control your new feet," he explained to the puzzled little hen. "There!" he said triumphantly. He set her down.

The little hen stood where he had placed her, peering queerly at her new, strange feet. The man laughed. "No, don't just stand and admire them—I'll do the admiring—you walk." He nudged her ahead. She promptly tipped forward. He set her up again. "Oh, it'll take lots of practice," he said encouragingly, and nudged her ahead.

But instead of trying to walk the little hen darted her beak with snakelike swiftness toward the flippers, seized the edge of a flipper, and tugged. She succeeded only in pulling herself over. The man set her back on her strange feet. Now, with a kernel of corn held before her beak, he tried to lure her into taking her first step. She stretched toward the corn, took a few steps, but cocked her head and stopped to listen to the strange clatter under her. Then, as she started toward the kernel of corn once more, she stepped on her own foot, and stood rocking back and forth on her crisscrossed rubber feet as if she were a nodding toy. The chuckling man unsnarled her feet for her.

In a far corner of the yard the rooster brought down an insect, clucked enticingly for his flock to come. The hens came running from everywhere. Forgetting her queer feet, the little hen started running with them. For a yard or two her speed somehow kept her upright, and she came clattering.

In the barnyard everything stopped. All heads twisted toward the little hen. For the moment the flock stood still in shocked alarm. Then the little hen tripped, slammed helplessly to the ground, lay kicking and thrashing her weird feet. The whole stupefied flock exploded into the air in a thundering mass of wings and feathers.

They crashed up against the walls of the barn and the hen house, smashed back to the ground, scrambled up, and scuttled away in desperate silence.

In one moment the barnyard was deserted, except for the little hen lying madly threshing her feet, in panic herself from the panic she had caused.

The man came to her in two long strides. Angrily he scooped her up. "Look what I did! We had them almost used to your knucklebones, and then I have to come with crazy rubber feet. And mind you—I thought I had something!"

He carried the little hen to the chair. He sat with her in the strange, silent emptiness of the deserted barnyard and became angry with himself all over again. "Frittering away my time, when I so seldom have a free hour. So I can't make artificial feet that'll take you up the ramp to the high coop, and keep you with the flock. But I *could* bring the coop down to you!"

He jerked startled eyes to the wide doorway of the cluttered basement of the big hay barn. "Hey, how come I never thought of that before? That useless basement's standing there full of old junk left from all the years, but I could change it into a hen house!" He hugged the little hen in his excitement. "A good, solid, snug hen house! And the floor would be on a level with the ground. You wouldn't have to climb anything, and the flock wouldn't freeze its combs and toes in there in winter." He cradled the little hen in his arm.

"Why, the basement of that big hay barn would be big enough for five hundred hens! But it would be an enormous big job to change it to a hen house, and I've so little free time from working on the big farm—" He pursed his lips. "But I could start!" he suddenly exploded. "You've got to start somehow, somewhere, with something. Just start!"

His excitement excited the little hen. She stretched up, peered at his shouting mouth. She forgot she was wearing rubber feet, and fluttered up to the man's shoulder. She couldn't balance there on her duck feet, had to beat her wings furiously to stay up at all. One wing fluttered in the man's face, startled him. "Hey, you're managing! Maybe everything isn't lost, after all— not even with my goofy rubber feet! Look, I've got an idea—you gave me an idea."

He hastily stripped the rubber flippers off the little hen's knucklebones, set her down on the chair, and raced to the house. When he returned, he had the two flippers securely pinned to the shoulder of his shirt. "See," he crowed. "See—now all I do is push your knucklebones down into the sockets, and you can ride on my shoulder just like always."

He pushed the little hen's knucklebones into the sockets of the pinned-down flippers. She rocked, started to use her wings, then sensed the new firmness, found she could balance. She folded her wings and nibbled excitedly at the man's cheek.

"See," the man crowed. "See!"

CHAPTER IV

Trap Door in the Ceiling

THE BIG hay barn across the barnyard from the horse barn with the high-loft chicken coop had been built into the side of a hill. The exposed stone wall of the basement of the hay barn with its little windows and wide doorway faced the barnyard, the other walls were buried in the cutaway hill. It had been built that way so that there would be windows for light for the cows that had once been kept in the basement of the barn and so that the door for the cows would be on a level with the flat ground of the barnyard.

But being built into a hill this way, the upper floor of the barn, where the hay for the cows had been stored, was on a level with the top of the hill, and so were the big hay doors on the opposite side of the barn. Thus there were two ways to get into the upper barn—from outside by way of the enormous hay doors, from the basement inside by way of a ladder and a trap door in the ceiling of the basement. The ceiling of the basement was, of course, the floor of the upper hay barn.

Since the big hay barn occupied the whole side of the little hill, the smaller horse barn, opposite it, had been built on level ground, so both floors of the horse barn were above the ground, not buried into the side of a hill. Therefore in this barn there was an inside stairway leading from the lower floor with the empty horse stables to the upper floor with its hen house. But the big hay barn had no inside stairway, just a ladder and trap door.

This is the way the barns had been built in the long-ago days, and this is the way the man had found them when he came to the farm. And except for building the makeshift chicken coop up in the horse barn, he had not changed anything at all. Since he worked on the big farm down the road, he had no use for the big barn—all he needed was the high-loft hen house in the small horse barn.

But in the old days this had once been a huge farm with herds of cows and teams of horses, and all the tools and machinery needed to work a big farm. When the farm was at last deserted, long years before the man had come, all the tools and machinery had been stored in the basement of the big barn. And there they still stood—cluttered and ancient and dusty and rusted. But now the man had decided to clear out the clutter, and rebuild the basement into a hen house. Being dug into the sheltering hill, a hen house in the basement of the barn would be snug and warm, the flock would not freeze combs and toes in such a hen house. What is more, the floor being on a level with the flat barnyard, the little red hen would not have to climb ramps, and in that way, even though toeless, she could stay with the flock.

It was an enormous project for the man, and maybe it had all come about because of a little hen's toelessness, but it was a good idea quite apart from that, for in the big basement the man could easily keep five hundred hens, and then he would have the beginnings of a poultry farm. And if he had a poultry farm, he would have independence, he wouldn't have to work for other farmers any more. That was the man's hope, and that his big plan. Just before noon he had got the idea. On the spur of the moment he had chosen to start his huge rebuilding project right after his noon-hour lunch. Just start!

But the big black dog that the man had twice taken away had chosen the cluttered basement of the barn as a good hiding place from the man. And sometime during the quiet noon hour of that free Monday, while the man was eating lunch, the big white rooster found the dog in the basement of the barn. The rooster almost stepped on him as he lay black and silent against the dark back wall of the barn. With shrill cackles the rooster whirled up and flapped away through the open doorway, but the dog skulked along the wall to find a darker, deeper hiding place. Against the end wall of the basement he found a double stack of bushel baskets. The towering baskets jiggled and tottered as he squeezed his big body behind them, but now the dog was satisfied. Now he lay facing the wide-open doorway.

He was back. Twice he'd been taken away, twice now he'd come back. And if the man were to take him away thirty times, he'd come back thirty times. He wasn't dim-witted—he knew he wasn't wanted here. But every time he was taken away, he'd try to come back. It wasn't a plan in the big dog's mind. It was a need, a desperation to have a home. He was going to have a home! It was that simple.

All by herself sometime during the noon hour the little red hen crossed the sunlit space of barnyard beyond the wide doorway. And suddenly the dog's tail slapped the bushel baskets a single hard slap. It boomed hollowly in the empty baskets. It scared the dog. He forced his tail still, but he couldn't prevent the delighted wriggle that shivered through his body. Just seeing the little red hen made him feel friendly and warm—safe almost, as if he, too, belonged. And in a way he belonged, for the little hen belonged to him. Hadn't he guarded her last night against everything that came? He remembered it proudly as he held himself absolutely still to keep himself from running to the little red hen.

The little red hen was the one thing that had brought the dog back. The other thing was the sure knowledge that the man was good. Whatever the man did to him, for whatever reason, the man was kind and good. And knowing that, the dog knew a sure fact: The little hen was his to guard and protect, and he was going to be the man's, and this was going to be his home.

He had known it early this morning when, after the long, confusing ride, the man had finally stopped the car at the side of a road and had said the familiar sounds and words again: "All right, poor old fellow, out you go. . . . Please do it quick."

Then the car had rattled away. The dog had stood at the side of the dark road with the memory in his ears of the hurried, sorrowful words of a man who did strange, unreasonable things but who was good. And knowing that surely, the dog had immediately taken off after the loud, rattling sounds of the car.

The man had really outwitted himself—not the dog. He had gone back by a roundabout way so as thoroughly to lose the dog this time. But the dog had not tried to follow the car down the roads at all. He had simply crossed fields and followed the rattling sounds of the car. Then, when the old car at last had gone into a drive leading to an enormous farm, the dog had not gone down the drive, but had waited in a deep roadside ditch before the farm.

Daylight had come, then sunlight, and then at last the old car had come back down the drive and had turned up the road to home. The dog had waited—not giving himself away by running on behind the car down an empty road—but almost with the man he had come home. Close by the barn, behind a clump of bushes, he had hid and waited. He'd been close enough to peer through the bushes and see the man with the little red hen in the rocking chair in the barnyard. And through him had gone a wriggle of warm delight.

His delight in the little red hen and the man had made the dog almost incautious. It had drawn him to the barn to be close to them, to belong, too, to be home. Then, as the man had sat poring over the mail-order catalog, the dog had stolen through the shadows along the barn wall and had slipped away into the darkness of the cluttered basement. He had done it in such creeping caution that he had not disturbed or alerted a single hen in the barnyard.

And now he was still in the barn, and it was noon. The little hen suddenly stepped from nowhere and hopped on her round knucklebones on to the doorsill of the wide doorway. The wriggle of delight shivered through the dog but stopped as it started, for suddenly in the sunlit doorway there also stood the man. The dog flattened. Sighting along his stretched-out paws, he silently, guardedly watched the two big feet planted in the doorway beside the little hen.

The noon hour was over.

The man started talking to the little hen. "Well, I definitely made up my mind over a can of sardines and a slice of bread—well, all right, six slices of bread—to change this basement into a hen house. No more loafing, no more whittling, no more rubber feet and holidays. Whatever little spare time I get, I'm going to use to clear this barn of all its junk."

He took a step forward, surveyed the crowded

clutter. "Gosh, it'll take weeks just to clear it.
And how I'm going to get it changed over into a
hen house before winter . . . It's a long aim,
little hen. Like laying your cheek along a long-
barreled rifle and sighting to nowhere. But I
guess all I can do is to start, see what comes."

He strode to a tall hay loader, the piece of
machinery closest to the doorway. He grabbed
up the tongue. The hay loader didn't stir,
wouldn't budge. "No wonder the old-time owners
left it near the door," the man grunted. But suddenly the steel wheels quickened in a grinding
sound over the cement floor, the towering machine
lurched forward, shot ahead, then stopped dead
against the doorsill.

The sudden motion threw the tugging man off
balance. He fell on his back outside the doorway.
He just let the heavy tongue rest on him, lay
staring up at the big, cumbersome machine.
"No," he gasped. "Oh, no."

The little red hen ran to him, excitedly peered
down into his face.

"You know what?" the man wearily told the
little hen. "That thing's too wide to go through
the doorway—too wide and too high." He

slowly arose. He rubbed a hand over his face, disgustedly eyed the hay loader. "You know what? I've got to push that big hulk back again; it blocks the whole doorway." His eyes went to the towering stacks of baskets where the dog lay hidden. "Now why couldn't I have started with something easy like those baskets?"

The wrenching struggle began again. But it was harder to push the hay loader than it had been to pull it. Then the man found that by twisting at the spokes of just one wheel he could turn the big hay loader in a half circle up against the wall beside the doorway. When at last it rammed against the wall the man was spent but triumphant. "Golly, look at it—almost reaches to that trap door in the ceiling. Well, now I'll try that seed drill back there. That's just a one-horse affair, and after moving that hay loader—if a horse can, I can."

But before tugging it out of its age-old place he lifted the lid and peered inside the seedbox of the drill. "Hey, still some old seed wheat in here!" He dug out a handful, looked at it. Wheat spilled from his hand and rolled over the floor. The little hen chased the wheat kernels. "You that hungry? Well, here . . ." The man sent the handful of wheat spraying across the barn. A hail of wheat hit the stacks of bushel baskets, bounced over the baskets, hit the wall, and showered down on the dog.

Pecking at the scattered wheat, following the trail of wheat, the little hen came around the stack of baskets, didn't see the motionless black dog in the darkness behind the baskets. She stepped over the dog's outstretched paw. One knucklebone just touched the hair of the paw. With a shrill cackle the little hen whirled and fluttered toward the doorway, just as the man came back from pulling the seed drill into the barnyard.

"Hey, what scared you?" But the man's mind was on his moving. "Golly, something easy this time—and not for a horse. Sure, a stack of baskets —baskets don't weigh. But I ought to stash them somewhere in the horse barn—I can use *them*."

He pulled away one of the stacks of baskets. Light fell into the dog's hiding place, but by not so much as the stir of a hair did the dog betray himself. The man creaked away with the tottering stack of baskets. But the little hen suddenly came around the remaining stack of baskets, stood peering at the motionless dog. She came a step closer, peered again, then, sure it was the dog, she darted right between his paws and pecked a kernel of wheat from under his shaggy chest. The dog did not move a muscle. The man was back. The man stood in the doorway.

The man surveyed the remaining clutter. "All right," he announced to no one. "Now that I've had a breather, that old wagon next." But when he got the unwieldy wagon outside, the front wheel caught in the deep rut made by the drip from the barn roof. The man talked wrathfully to the stubborn wagon wheel. "Well, all right, then, if you won't jump that rut, stay in it! I'll just have to pull the whole wagon along the rut and the wall and leave it under the drip."

He came back panting, sweat rolling down his face. "That mule of a wagon calls for a breather again," he announced. "Time for a nice light stack of baskets . . . The old barn is clearing, though."

The height of the stack of baskets as he lifted them kept the man from seeing the dog. This time the dog did not wait. The moment the man was over the doorsill, the dog crept along the wall. The little hen followed him. The dog edged toward the doorway, stood listening, as if trying to decide whether or not to dash out into the bright sunlit barnyard and around the barn and out of sight. The little hen behind him stood looking up—fascinated by the dust rays sifting and sparkling in a bar of sunlight that came streaming down through the slightly open trap door above the leaning rack of the hay loader.

A tuft of hay caught between the edge of the door and the floor of the upper barn held the trap door partly open and let the sunlight stream through. The little hen stood entranced by the shimmering dust rays.

From the horse barn came a surge of song. The dog stiffened, looked uncertainly back at the little hen, then he, too, looked up at the trap door. Now the song burst loud as the man came singing across the barnyard, but then stopped to talk to the chickens. The dog whirled, mounted the rack of the hay loader, dragged himself up by the ropes and slats of the leaning hayrack. The loading rack swayed and groaned with the struggles of the dog. Then his nose was at the opening of the trap door. He hunched head and shoulders, thrust up at the trap door, forced it up. With hindlegs feeling and poking for support on the unsteady hayrack, the dog slid his front paws over the floor above. He dragged himself up by his forelegs. The tuft of hay that had held the trap door open fell down in the struggle. Up above, the trap door eased down as the dog slid from under it. With a tiny thud it fell shut.

Above the trap door the big dog lay exhausted in the dusty hay he had pushed up in his struggles. Suddenly he sneezed because of hay dust in his nostrils. After the sneeze he lay frozen, listening. But the grinding sound of iron wheels over the concrete basement floor came up to his ears. Reassured, the big dog padded away, found some piled hay in a corner, and crawled behind the hay.

The barn was warm with sun. Bars and stripes of light coming through the chinks between the long upright boards of the barn wall lay over the floor and the hay. The emptiness of the huge barn, its warmth, its silence, its dusty smell, seemed to bring the dog assurance—made him feel he was safe. There wasn't a single scent of

use—not the faintest scent that the man had ever been here. The dog sneezed again, but the sneeze was muffled in the hay pile into which he had sunk. He wearily closed his eyes, felt safe enough not to be alert—safe enough, after all his exertion, to sleep a little.

A loud yell from the barnyard roused the dog. Immediately alert, he was also immediately on guard. Only his ears pricked up, otherwise he did not move. He lay listening. The man was yelling down in the barnyard.

"Come on, little hen," the man yelled once more. "It's way past milking time on the big farm. But I've got to put you under that potato crate before I go. I've got to know you're safe. Come on, girl."

Sure of the safety and secrecy of his new surroundings, the dog padded over to the wall of the barn, peered through a chink between two of the long up-and-down boards. The man stood in the barnyard in the midst of all the clutter he had dragged out of the basement. White hens were around him, fluttering up among the tall machinery, pecking curiously at all the strange things. The man paid them no attention. He scrunched down, peered and searched among the clutter. "Come on," he called out again, "you're only bringing trouble on yourself—it'll be dark soon." He shrugged his shoulders helplessly, turned, and ran from the barnyard. Moments later the old car rattled away down the road.

In the high barn the dog listened to the last rattles of the old car as he peered through the

chink into the deep barnyard. The sun had set,
and the night was early, but the chickens were
earlier. Already the first ones trudged determin-
edly up the long ramp. Out of the high hen house
came the squawking and quarreling of the nightly
fight for an exact, favorite spot on the roost. The
sound alerted the hens still on the ground; they,
too, hurried up the ramp.

Below the watching dog the barnyard lay still
and deserted; nothing stirred among its clutter.

Then into the barnyard came the little red hen on her quick rolling gait. She tried to scamper up the ramp. But she slid back, and flopped to the ground. She stumbled up, tried it right over again, slid again.

The rooster poked his head out of the opening at the top of the ramp. There, fluttering about at the bottom of the ramp, and not coming up at all, was the little red hen. He strode on to the ramp, warned the little hen to come up. She just kept fluttering and flapping her wings, didn't obey, didn't come up. The rooster grimly watched her with no understanding.

Offended by this disobedience, the rooster pelted down to the ground, tried to drive the little hen up the ramp. She staggered up before him, but lost her balance, knocked his proud feet from under him. Together the scared little hen and the enraged rooster flopped to the ground.

The little hen was up first. She scuttled across the barnyard, racing for the deep shadows against the wall of the looming hay barn. The rooster took after her in grim silence. He, too, disappeared in the shadows.

Up in the barn the dog stiffened, lunged away

from the wall, raced toward the big doors on the opposite side of the barn. He threw himself against them, but he could not budge them. Now there was a pained squawk from the little hen in the barnyard. At the sound the dog turned from the doors, raced back toward the opposite wall. Too late he tried to brake himself. He skidded, slid headlong in the loose hay, crashed against one of the long boards in the wall. Outside, rusted heads of old nails gave, spat out of the board. The end of the board flew out from the floor. The dog plunged down. But the heavy board sprang back, caught the dog's hindquarters in a painful grip, held him. The dog hung head down against the outside wall of the barn.

Right below him stood the old wagon where the man had left it. The little hen had hidden in the wagon box, sat squeezed in a corner. But now the rooster flew up to the wagon.

Suddenly the springy board in the wall let the dog free. He plunged into the wagon box. The wagon rocked. The scared rooster squawked up in startled flight, but the dog's vengeful jaws caught a tip of the rooster's wing. The rooster jerked and squawked and struggled. The smooth feathers slipped from between the dog's teeth. The rooster tumbled away over the side of the wagon box.

Over the rim of the wagon box the dog watched the rooster run in scared silence toward the ramp. He did not follow. He turned, looked at the corner where the little hen sat meekly looking up at him. She was too hurt to move. The big dog flopped himself down beside her, and he thoughtfully licked at his own wounds. And they two were quiet together in the deep, safe darkness of the wagon box as the evening deepened into night.

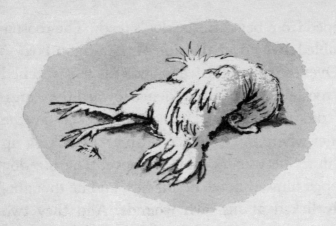

CHAPTER V

Parsnips

IT WAS the end of the week that had begun with the Sunday-Monday holiday and the clearing of the basement of the barn. It was Saturday. The man opened the kitchen door. The little hen was waiting for him on the doorsill. The man finished putting on his jacket and picked her up. "It beats me, little hen, but every morning there you are again—safe and sound, and all in one piece. How you manage to live through the nights with all that comes out of the big swamp to roam this farm at night—gosh, there's even foxes in that swamp—I can't figure out. Without toes you sure

can't roost up high, and why something doesn't get you wherever you hide out on the ground . . . Well, they haven't found you yet. And it's fine, if it lasts."

He suddenly tapped the shoulder of his jacket. "See that? I don't know how you manage to stay alive, but I'm betting on you to last. So last night I sewed your flippers on this jacket—permanently." He snickered. "If yesterday I didn't catch myself rushing into the barn on the big farm with your rubber flippers still pinned to my shirt! Boy, if the boss had seen that! . . . Well, I suppose it is kind of goofy—flippers on the shoulder. But now all I have to remember is to take the jacket off before I rush off to the big farm." He planted the little hen's knucklebones in the sockets.

A sudden storm of cackling out of the high hen house made the man put a supporting hand over the little hen and run for the horse barn. At the top of the stairway he took the precaution to knock on the door so as not to panic the flock once more. Then he opened the door. The whole flock rushed to him, crowded around him, eyes excited and flickery and alert. But the man waded through the flock. From the water fountain stand hung a hen. She hung upside down, caught by one foot. The bloodied white hen hung limp and still, wings fallen open. The caught hen had obviously slammed against the ceiling in her panic, then in her fall had trapped her foot in a brace of the stand, and there she'd hung, helplessly upside down. And it being odd for a chicken to hang upside down—it being queer, different, the flock had turned on her to destroy her.

The man pulled her free, examined her. "You silly fools," he said angrily. "You cannibals! The moment one of you is helpless, all of you turn on her. And where were you?" he suddenly shouted at the rooster. "Helping to rip her to pieces, I suppose, when you should have protected her. You and your evil, stupid little brain!" He strode to the opening in the wall, yanked up the slide door. "Out!" he yelled. "Out. Roam the fields, find your own food. That'll keep you busy. That'll leave you no time for deviltry."

The white hens poured through the opening, slid and fluttered and ran happily down the long ramp. The big rooster strutted past the man, crowded toward the opening among his streaming flock. Suddenly the man kicked out at him.

The little red hen on his shoulder chose that moment to nibble excitedly at the man's cheek. It startled the man. "Hey," he said, calming down, "it gets you at times—so much stupidity. And so much meanness because of the stupidity. Hey," he exclaimed suddenly, "I'm no better:

I'm ashamed—kicking at that rooster. Maybe the chickens were acting human . . . But I've got to get to the big farm—I'm late."

He hurried down the stairs with the white hen in his arms and the little red hen bobbing on his shoulder. "The hay barn," he suddenly told the white hen. "That's where I'll put you—up in the hay barn. The flock can't get at you there. Then tonight I'll wash off the dried blood so it won't attract those cannibals to you again."

He grabbed up a handful of grain on his way out of the horse barn, ran to the pump, and filled a coffee can with water. He tugged the bottom corner of one of the big double doors away from the wall, held it with his knee, reached in, and shoved the grain, coffee can, and the white chicken inside. He ran for the car. The little hen teetered on his shoulder, balancing herself the best she could. One wing slid over the man's nose as he stooped to get in the car. "Hey, forgot you in the excitement. Imagine me coming on the big farm with you on my shoulder!"

He tugged the little hen out of the rubber sockets and set her on the ground. But she hopped and fluttered up against his leg, wanting to be put back. The man grinned down at her. "No, you can't come along. But tomorrow's Sunday, tomorrow's my free day—and hanged if I don't take time from clearing that barn tomorrow to find out where you keep yourself nights. It can't last—that swamp's too close."

He pulled his jacket off, wadded it, and threw it in the back of the car. "Golly, if you'd only change your little game—wait for me at the kitchen door evenings instead of mornings. I've even got a box behind the stove with straw and everything—you could sleep in there, then I'd know you were safe. But tomorrow I'll try to find out. Got to go now—I'm way late."

In the big, high-vaulted barn the white hen sat for a moment exactly where the man had shoved her. Then she stood up, head high, neck twisting in alarm, eyes flicking to all points in the great, hushed, enclosed space. Barred sunlight striped through the chinks between the long upright boards in the walls. Barred shadows stretched over the floor. Silently the hen began wading high-legged through the layers of hay. Then she ran; ran faster, faster until she pummeled herself up in blind squawking flight. She hurtled against the wall where sunlight striped through the chinks. She fell back, landed in some piled hay in a corner.

The pile of hay exploded under her. In paralyzed surprise the hen sat sunken in hay, looking glassy-eyed at the huge black dog that had burst up from the hay. The dog looked strangely at the chicken. For a moment they stood motionless before each other. Then a single alarmed cluck welled up in the chicken. She began clucking, clucking—and as if the clucking wound her up, she marched again, stalked again, ran. Ran, flew, flew up in a wild welter of cacklings, as if propelling herself up on great squalls of cackles. She landed on a big crossbeam, high against the peaked roof. She paced there, head bobbing, clucking—telling herself hysterical things about the scary huge dog in this strange, silent, huge place.

From far down the road came the fading rattle of the old car. The dog pricked up his ears, listened to the faint sounds. He stood quiet, but he was shaken. It had been a close call when the man had suddenly jerked the door away from the wall and had shoved a handful of corn and a coffee can with water at him. It had been a close call, but not a total surprise. From the time the man had stepped out of the kitchen door and picked up the little hen, the dog had followed the man's every move by following the walls of the barn and peering through the chinks between the boards.

But the big hay doors were solid. And when the man had come from the pump he had been out of view of the dog. Then the man had suddenly jerked at the doors and his hand had stretched toward the dog. There hadn't been a moment to lose. On a silent lope the dog had gone across the barn and had plunged into the hay for hiding. But the man had not come. Now the car was rattling away, and there was only the clucking chicken.

Paying no further attention to the hen on the beam, the dog trotted back to the doors. He lapped up the water in the coffee can, then he hungrily bit into the grain. He cracked the grain kernels under hard teeth. The chicken stared nervously down at the sounds of his eating.

Behind the dog there was a dull plop and the

sound of a splatter. The dog whipped around. On the high beam the terrified hen had laid an egg. Now, without a single cackle coming from her, she stood neck stretched down, peering in stupid surprise at the fallen shattered egg. The dog trotted over and sniffed at an egg splatter on a tuft of hay. Then eagerly he wolfed the egg, hay dust and all. He hunted up the pieces of eggshell and crunched them between his teeth. Then there was no more.

The dog looked up at the chicken. He looked at the spot where the egg had splattered, stood as if thinking. He looked up at the chicken again, and now his tail waved. He had made a great discovery—chickens laid eggs, and eggs were food, tasty food. And food was his problem— the everlasting, everyday problem.

The dog had made this place his home, but there was no food for him in his adopted, stolen home. There wasn't even a tossed-out table scrap—the man ate most of his meals at the big farm. And the man did not know he was here. The man set out food for the little red hen under a staked-down crate at the kitchen door, because the little hen could not climb the ramp to the food in the hoppers in the hen house. The man had made the crate with an opening at one end too small for the bigger white hens and far too small for the dog's big head. There had been days of this week when the dog had lain flat before the small opening in the potato crate as the little hen ate inside the crate. And sometimes, in a shamed, puppyish whine, he had begged the little hen under the crate for a morsel of chicken food.

But now the dog settled himself firmly on his haunches, sat in the hay under the high beam, waiting for the chicken to lay another egg for him.

Other mornings he would have waited only long enough for the last rattle of the car to die away down the road, then he would have lunged at the loosened board in the wall, would have lowered himself down the outside wall, would have dropped headlong to the wagon box, and leaped to the ground to eat scattered grain with the chickens. Because of the little red hen, the man had started a new custom—instead of tossing the grain into the straw of the high hen house, he had taken to scattering it over the barnyard, so that the little hen could eat with the flock.

From the first morning the dog had made shrewd use of the man's new way of feeding the flock. But it took time to get down from the barn.

By the time the dog had waited for the old car and had made his painful way down from the barn, the flock had already picked up most of the grain. He had to pick up the leavings. He roved and ranged and scrounged with the flock, a big black dog among white chickens, searching busily for grain beside the little hen. With his keen nose he'd learned to smell out hid-

den grain kernels. Even then the little red hen, quick and darting, often pecked up the kernel from under his nose. But the big starved dog would not growl or snap at her, he was her protector.

The dog sat patiently waiting for the high hen to lay another egg. This morning he was in no hurry. He knew that the man had driven the hens out of the hen house, and had scattered no grain for the flock.

It was a lean life. Pickings and scroungings, and single kernels of grain for his huge, hungry body. Yesterday, in the desperation of his hunger, the dog had turned to the fenced-in garden beside the house. Having learned to climb the ropes and tangled slats of the sagging rack of the hay loader to the trap door in the ceiling, he had taught himself to climb the woven wire fence into the garden.

But it was a last year's garden, and only a few old tomatoes—winter frozen and spring rotted— had still lain there. He'd bitten one, and he'd found it repulsive. But then he'd found a row of parsnips that had been left in the ground over the winter. He'd found the parsnips brittle and hard and sweet—in a faint, farfetched way, almost as sweet and crunchy as a bone. He had pulled up the parsnips one by one, and he'd lain down with them, gnawing them, chiseling them with sharp front teeth as he would a good bone. And for the first time in a week his stomach had felt firm and full.

Later he had rested in the hayloft of the barn, and along his tongue had lingered the sweetness of the full feeling—the brave, sure feeling of enough food. And it was decent and good.

Oh, it was no life for a dog—this chicken life among chickens. But it was a life, and it was a home, even though it was a stolen home.

And now it had been his life for almost a week. Daily his new life began when the last rattle of the old car faded away down the road; it ended in the evening when the old car came rattling back. The rest of his life was hiding. When the car brought the man home, the dog went into hiding. He set his time by the sounds of the car. The old rattletrap car was his alarm clock.

The dog's half-hidden life had begun when in his desperation he had climbed the hay loader and pushed through the trap door to the upper barn. By doing so he had found himself the best hiding place he possibly could have found anywhere on the little farm. And even if it had come by accident, it was shrewd of the dog that he continued to use his hiding place.

It had also been by accident that the dog had lunged across the barn, and skidded and crashed against the board in his attempt to get to the rooster and the little hen. But it was shrewd of the dog that he continued to use the loosened board.

With a way to get in and a way to get out, the upper hay barn had worked out as the perfect hiding place, the only place where the man never came. But through every chink between the boards along the walls the dog could watch the man.

The rattles of the old car were the dog's warning by day. The lights of the house were his guide by night. When the lights at last went out in the house, the dog would come out of hiding and drop down from the barn to the old wagon to sleep with and protect the little hen in the wagon box through the night. Fortunately the little hen always awoke at the crack of dawn to hurry to wait for the man at the kitchen door. Then the dog would jump down from the wagon, too, and hurry into hiding for an hour or two until the time came when the old car once again rattled away to take the man to work for the day on the big farm down the road.

If all this fitted into a plan, it was a simple, single plan—the dog was going to have a home. It was that simple, it was that great.

But now the dog sat patiently waiting for the white hen up on the high beam to lay another egg for him. Outside the barn there was a pained squawk from the little red hen in the barnyard. In his week the dog had learned to distinguish that sound from all the other barnyard sounds. He lunged toward the loosened board.

CHAPTER VI

The Dog and the Rooster

THE BIG DOG crashed against the bottom of the loosened board, and drove it away from the wall. He plunged through the opening.

Down below, at his crashing lunge, everything stopped in the barnyard. But in the week the chickens had become used to the dog plunging down into the wagon box. The next moment in the barnyard everything went on as before.

In the midst of a group of white chickens the little red hen was in a hen fight for some hen reason. The crash of the dog had interrupted the fight, but now the little hen leaped up at her white enemy again. The fight resumed where it had left off.

The fight was mean, unfair, one-sided. While the little red hen was fighting one white hen, other white hens darted in and pecked her. The little hen, blinded with rage, chugging with frustrated rage, leaped up, raked at the puffed white chest before her with her useless, harmless knucklebones. The whole group closed in on her. The little hen went down squawking, buried under white hens.

In the wagon the dog looked down at it. But in hitting the wagon box the dog had twisted his paw. He had to sink down a moment, bite and lick at his own hurt.

The rooster heard the squawking, came around the barn on a run. The white hens scattered, and there was only the little hen sprawled in the dust. The rooster charged at her, rapped her viciously —as if beating her for having got herself beaten. The little hen croaked out a wretched squawk. At that sound the dog leaped out of the wagon and ran to the little hen. He ran right over the rooster, knocked him sprawling. The rooster picked himself up, pushed past the dog and ran up the ramp to sulk in the hen house.

The big dog, plume tail waving in friendliness and greeting, touched his nose to the little red hen, and she raised her head and looked up at him. He nuzzled her again, but they really had no way of showing their friendship. But here he was now, their day together could begin. The chickens that had scuttled away came back— the normal barnyard life was resumed.

The little red hen got up, shook the leftover pain out of her hurt comb, saw an insect flitting along in the shadows under the hulking machinery in the barnyard, and gave chase. Tail waving, the big dog loped after her.

Side by side the big dog and the little hen ranged the barnyard. They roved about the barn and the hen house, scrounging along the walls for hidden grain kernels and chicken tidbits. The little hen picked up things, tested them for food taste, rejected or gobbled them. The dog tagged on behind.

The pickings were lean this hungry morning. The man in his rage had kicked the flock out of the hen house to fend for themselves and had not scattered grain for them in the barnyard. He had even forgotten to fill the cake tin underneath the potato crate for the little red hen. Patiently with the little hen—she forgot in a few moments—the dog made three useless trips to the empty potato crate at the kitchen door.

Back in the barnyard the dog sniffed out a kernel of corn stuck under the curved tooth of a harrow—one kernel for his huge, hungry body. He flopped to his side, rooted like a pig, to force the kernel free. The little hen darted in, greedily pecked up the kernel the dog had freed. The dog got up, looked at her, and accepted it meekly. But the tip of his tail wavered in a wistful question.

The little hen darted away. The dog hopefully poked his nose under the harrow once more, but the little hen squawked and he pulled himself free, hurried to her. It was all that was needed. The white hen pecking the little red hen scuttled away.

The two stood together again. The dog looked longingly across the field at the distant swamp. His tail began waving, brushed the little hen. Then he started forward on a determined lope into the field and whatever it might hold for him by way of food. The little hen ran with him. But she ran only so far from the barnyard, then, frightened by the strangeness, she uttered a single quick cackle, turned, and fluttered back. The dog stood looking at her, tail waving in indecision, but then he trotted after her. He had made himself her unquestioning slave. He stayed with the little red hen. It was his life. He was there to protect her and to put a quick end to her eternal fights. It was his duty. He had made it his duty.

The little hen did not know, could not accept, or could not remember that her new place was at the very bottom of the flock. By some inexorable flock code she had been shoved down to the number one hundred position—the last and the least of all the flock since she had lost her toes. And since she was at the very bottom, all the others had the right to lord it over her, peck and maul and bully her. That the little hen would not, or could not, accept. When they pecked her she fought, and when she fought she lost—toeless she was harmless. But always she fought again.

Only the big rooster was still somewhat impartial. When she fought with another hen, he separated the two impartially with a slashing blow or two with the side of his hard bill. But always he seemed to rap the little hen harder. Always he seemed to knock her down.

The big dog ignored the rooster, and the rooster ignored him, except when the rooster from some rooster instinct stepped in to punish the little hen for fighting. That the big dog would not allow. He did not snap or snarl at the rooster— he simply walked him down. And the rooster nearly always remembered to keep his distance. He seemed to sense that the big dog had little patience with him; he seemed to accept the fact that the dog had made himself a sort of rooster-protector to the little hen.

It was the new life the dog had established for himself. He was the little hen's protector, and he was her slave. He loved it. It gave him a purpose and a duty. He loved it maybe more than he loved the little red hen.

If the little hen did not sense it or accept it, in some dim way the dog seemed to understand that by the code of the flock he and the little hen were really outcasts, and if not quite outcasts— since he was too big and powerful—at least they were outsiders. More and more the big dog tried to lead the little hen away from the flock into the fields beyond the barnyard. More and more the little hen—tired of constant peckings, and of being eternally bullied—tended to follow him away from the flock. But the strangeness, the wideness and emptiness of the stretching fields always scared her back to the barnyard. She would step along beside the dog only up to such a point. Then panic and alarm would overtake her and she would tear back to the busy barnyard, away from the big silence of the field. The dog would patiently trot after her.

But the man in his morning rage, by not feeding the flock, and by kicking them out to scrounge food for themselves, had unwittingly changed it all. There was nothing more to be found in the pecked-over barnyard. There was no food in the hen house feed hoppers. Hungry and restless, the flock began to stray farther and farther afield. Hunger made them dare to step out under the high, empty sky over the flat, silent field. And the big dog led them. And the little hen walked at his side.

The flock did not follow very far. The chickens

spread over the near field, but they stayed in groups and tight little clusters. Like the little hen, they reached a certain point in the big strangeness where they would suddenly lift heads in alarm, eye the high sky, and then in wild, cackling fright race back to the barnyard. When one started for the barn, the others would catch her panic, and chickens would bolt from everywhere. Gradually they would edge into the field again, but the presence of hawks over the swamp, the fear of hawks, kept the hens close to the barnyard.

The little hen had gone too far into the field. Once, in panic, she turned from the dog, and made a short, hurtling flight back. But when her flight ended, and she stumbled down in the grass, she saw that the big barn still looked far away. The dog was near. The dog waited for her. She ran back to the dog, and he led the way to the swamp again.

From the swamp came a whirring and sawing of thousands of hidden insects. The mysterious swamp stirred, weed tops waved, bushes sighed and bent. A wind swept the tall plumes of high swamp grasses, bent them toward the little hen, and to the little hen it was as if the whole waving reed field flowed toward her like water, and would engulf her. She stood paralyzed, eyes glazed. Then, when the wind passed, she noticed that the dog had trudged on, and to her it seemed as if the dog had gone under in the waves of bowing reeds.

At the edge of the swamp an old willow had fallen, had gone on growing, its leaves and limber branches hanging only inches from the ground. Far behind the little hen, faint over the field, came the rooster's hawk warning—from the top of the ramp the rooster was warning of hawks. At that sound the lone little hen panicked. She flew toward the willow, plunged to the ground and scurried under the tipped-down branches of the fallen willow.

Under the low, leaning trunk of the willow tree, she found a depression in the ground. She squeezed herself down into the cupped hollow. The leaves of the tipped-down branches curtained around her, shut out the sight of the swamp. They even seemed to dim the shrillness of insects. The little hen felt securely hidden. Panic seeped out of her. She began fussing with

the cupped hollow to shape it more to her liking. She tugged a few weed stalks and some dead grass around her body, and now it was a nest. A secret, hidden, dark nest! And now she wanted to lay an egg in the most hidden nest. The little hen became quiet. The time had come to lay an egg.

The dog had plunged into the waving, shoulder-high, plumy grass, because there had been a trail and a smell of some small animal. It spelled food. Absorbed in the scent before his nose, he hurried on. But the trail was lost in wateriness that stood at the roots of the reeds and the grasses. The dog still splashed on. Suddenly, beyond the reeds, he plunged into the deeper swamp—a long, twisting sheet of stagnant, still water. Slithery things stirred in the shallow water at the swamp's edge, squirmed, flashed, wriggled.

The dog plunged into the swamp in pursuit of whatever moved there. He bit the water, but always whatever skittered and wriggled in the shallows flashed away into deeper water. The hungry dog became shrewd, splashed no more, but stood still, paws motionless. Something wriggled against a paw—a tiny crayfish. The dog lunged, snapped . . . it was small, it squirmed about his teeth, but the dog gave it a hard bite, a quick taste, and swallowed. Suddenly he looked back to where the big barn must rise behind the fringe of trees and brush. It was as if the small, quick taste reminded him of something. And then the dog knew—the crayfish had faintly tasted like the egg the chicken in the barn had dropped down to him from the high beam.

He immediately left the swamp. He trotted faster and faster. Near the willow he circled a moment, found the spot from which the little red hen had fluttered up, but there her track ended. The dog hurried on to the barn.

The little red hen had heard the dog circling and sniffing, but she had stayed silent and secret in the nest under the leaning trunk of the willow. Sure of herself in the great importance of laying an egg, she let the dog rustle away across the field.

In the barnyard the dog ran straight for the open doorway of the basement of the barn. He hurriedly climbed the sagging hay loader, shoved himself up through the trap door. The white hen was in the hay on the barn floor. The dog ran to her. The chicken stood paralyzed, eyes glassy with alarm, as the dog stopped expectantly before her. But her eyes flicked to the dog's shaggy, wet coat. She darted her beak at the dog, stripped away a drop of water. At the taste of water she boldly pushed in, pecked up at the dog's dripping chest—too thirsty to be afraid. She pulled hairs. It nipped, it stung. Almost carelessly the dog opened his big mouth and closed it over her back. A hoarse squawk squeezed out of the chicken. At that squawk the dog immediately dropped her. She scuttled away.

The dog threw himself down. He swiped a tongue over his chops as if to examine the taste of the chicken, but he had not bitten down, and there was only a dry feather taste in his mouth. He licked at his wet fur to get rid of the dead taste. He fell asleep licking his fur.

The flock had wandered off into the field again. The rooster stood alone on the high ramp, watching, listening—worried and concerned. The barnyard lay empty below the ramp. A single sparrow flew down from the roof of the barn. The rooster ducked, but then he used the sparrow's flight as an excuse to warn his flock of hawks. Once again he whirred out his alarm warnings—hawks overhead. From everywhere in the near field hens rose, thrashed in clumsy flight toward the barnyard.

The rooster stood high and silent and important on the ramp looking down on his scared flock. But having been warned of non-existent hawks once too often, the flock began to doubt the rooster. They had made too many useless flights back to the barnyard. They cocked eyes to the empty sky, saw nothing threatening. The seeds and insects in the field beckoned. There was food in the field; the flock scattered again.

From the ramp the frustrated rooster whirred a useless alarm call after them—hawks overhead. The flock paid him no attention. On the ramp the rooster wound himself into a hateful rage. But there was no hen near to vent his rage on. Feeling foolish, feeling useless, the rooster stood confused and alone on the high ramp.

In the barn the dog awoke. He got up, searched for a splattered egg. There was no egg. The chicken was busy scratching among the hay for hay seeds. The dog ran to the loosened board in the wall and plunged down.

The crash of the dog alarmed the lone rooster on top of the ramp. With a hoarse squawk he flew down from the ramp, and ran toward his scattered flock in the field. Alone in the barnyard, the hungry dog searched for grain kernels. There was nothing to be found. In the hen house a chicken cackled. The dog trotted to the basement of the hay barn as if the cackling had made him hopeful that the imprisoned white hen might have laid an egg for him.

Under the hay loader in the tuft of hay that had fallen down from the trap door a chicken had made a nest. There were three eggs in the partly concealed nest. The dog picked up an egg. His teeth closed on it. The egg crashed and splashed in his mouth, its sweetness oozed over his tongue. The tip of the dog's tail waved gratefully. He reached for the second egg.

In the field the rooster rolled out a hawk warning. The warning shut itself off abruptly as the rooster himself ducked into a clump of weeds. This time the warning was real. The hens in the field sensed it. Now there was no hysteria, no panic, no flight. All over the field the hens became flattened white lumps, frozen into motionlessness under any grass tuft or weed clump. Overhead a hawk flew, flew low, looking down on the field with brazen, bold eyes. Suddenly the hawk chose to fly on, sailed high, flew away in busy swiftness, and was gone from the sky.

The rooster stood up. He called to his hens—threatening, coaxing, commanding. They all ran flat-tailed through the grass toward home and the safety of the barnyard. The rooster drove them on with his warnings and orders.

Behind the rooster—far behind him from the looming brush edge of the swamp—came a shrill cackling. It went on and on. The little hen had laid an egg in the secret, hidden nest under the willow. Now she cackled and cackled shrill triumph beyond the tree.

The rooster wheeled, rolled out his alarm calls to her. He coaxed, he called, he ordered. The little hen did not listen. She ran back and forth cackling the magnificent event of the egg up to the sky. A bluebird flew over the field, reminding the rooster of hawk dangers again.

In the field all the scuttling flock had stopped at the familiar homey sounds of the little hen's cackling. Hawk forgotten, chickens raised their heads and stood listening to the distant shrill song of the little hen. They started back into the field.

The rooster warned direly of the bluebird. No one believed him, no one paid any attention. The rooster went berserk with rage. In hate and frustration he charged toward this farthest-away, most obstinate little hen of all his flock.

The little hen saw him coming, and so that he would not discover her secret nest, she ran to him. But when she reached him, the rooster knocked her down, thrashed her unmercifully. She struggled up and tried to skulk away in the deep grass; he overtook her and beat her down again. Overhead a dot-high hawk, hurrying to the home nest with a mouse in its talons, swept a bold eye down to the scene of the fearful beating. For a moment the hawk circled, hovered, but then decided to fly on with the small prize already in its possession.

Completely unaware of the hawk, the rooster in blood-blinded rage went on thrashing the little hen. She slipped from under him, tried to squeeze away toward the willow. But the rooster came down on her and the little hen squawked.

In the barn the dog heard the distant squawk above the crunching sound of the second egg he was shattering under his teeth. He grabbed the last egg, pulled it into his mouth. Again the little hen squawked. Egg still in his mouth, the dog whirled and ran toward the sound.

The rooster was insanely hammering the little hen. His wings were spread with the effort. His beak gaped in his wheezing. Little tiny fluff feathers clung to the sides of his bill. Still he thrashed her.

Then the big dog was there, silent, ominous. He opened his mouth, let the egg roll, snatched

the rooster up and away from the little red hen—
held him high, shook him savagely. One wing
slipped from the dog's hold, beat wildly in the
dog's face, blinded him. The dog dropped the
rooster for a new hold. In silent terror the rooster
scuttled away, flew up, bolted up toward the faraway safety of the hen house and barn. But he had
to land after his desperate short flight, and when
he stumbled down the dog was there. The hapless
rooster flew up again, stumbled down, ran in wit-

less, wing-pumping panic before the silent dog. Always the dog was under or behind him. The rooster ran out before him, mouth gaping, his breath coming out of his open beak in hoarse, pained gasps. He somehow forced himself up into a last short flight, but he could hardly raise himself above the weed stalks.

At last the rooster felt the familiar packed ground of the barnyard. He stumbled toward the ramp. The ramp was crowded with chickens. The rooster wobbled away again, staggered up the rise from the deep barnyard to the yard of the house. He managed to squirm around the corner of the house, squatted there, wheezing painfully, eyes closed.

The dog poked his nose around the corner of the house. In the desperate strength of terror, the rooster hurled up, flew into the unseen chicken wire around the little parsnip garden. He caught his neck in an opening of the chicken wire, uttered a deep squawk, thrashed his wings, hung still.

The dog came trotting up. He reared up, leaned against the fencing, and sniffed at the dead rooster. Then to his ears came the first rattle of the old car from far down the road. The dog dropped to the ground, hurried away to hide in the barn.

In the far field the beaten little hen heard the old car come rattling. She raised her head, and saw the white egg the dog had dropped in the grass. Forgetting her hurt, she got up and immediately began fussing with the egg. She hooked her bill behind it, pulled it free of the grass tufts, rolled the egg toward her secret nest under the willow tree. She worked the egg over the rim of the nest until at last, with a faint click, it rolled down beside her own egg. Then the little hen settled herself on the two eggs. She clucked little motherly sounds at the two lovely eggs under her. She was proud of her eggs, and her hurt was forgotten.

The man saw the rooster the moment he stepped from the car. He hurried over, pulled the dead rooster out of the fencing, felt that he was still warm. He felt under the rooster's feathers. Hastily he began to pluck the still-warm carcass, stripping the feathers away. Again he examined the rooster. And now he found bite marks, tiny sharp punctures in the one wing. The man shook his head. "Something bit him all right, but that bite wasn't enough to kill him. It looks as though he tore away from whatever bit him, and then got chased into the fence and broke his neck. But, then, why didn't whatever chased him take the rooster away?" He looked at the leaning, sagging fencing. "Maybe," the man guessed aloud, "whatever it was got scared away by my coming. If this isn't a queer mystery!"

But then—pasted to the side of the rooster's bloodied bill—he saw the tiny red fluff feathers of the little hen. The man ran to the barnyard, looked around for the little hen. She was not among the few hens in the barnyard, but now the rest of the flock came down from the hen house, crowded around the man, and began a hungry humming. "Sure, I know—you're starved. But I forgot to put out food for the little hen, too, and she isn't here. Wait until I dress this rooster, then I'll feed you in the coop, and lock you up for the night."

At the pump the man grabbed a pail, threw the rooster's carcass in it, and pumped cold water over it. Suddenly he listened. Above and beyond the impatient, hungry hen sounds humming up from the barnyard, from far over the swamp a hawk screamed in the evening stillness. Distant and thin as it was, the cry came proud, eerie, vengeful.

"Hawks!" the man exclaimed. "I don't know," he said down to the rooster in the pail, "if now with you gone the hawks will stay over the swamp. That's one thing you did perfectly, you grim fool—warn and protect the flock from hawks."

A small red feather came gently rising to the surface of the water in the pail. The man looked at it. "You got what you had coming," he said softly to the dead rooster. "My thanks to whatever did it. If it hadn't, I'd have killed you for killing my little hen."

The hawk screamed again above the swamp. "Hey—you don't suppose the hawks got the little hen—maybe after you beat her half to death?" The man stood listening. "I'll feed the flock, and then I'll take the flashlight and go looking for her in the swamp," he suddenly decided. "Or for whatever killed her," he added grimly.

CHAPTER VII

The Little Boss

WHEN THE MAN decided to go searching for the little hen in the darkening swamp, he unknowingly held the big dog trapped up in the hay barn. The dog could not come out of hiding—not with the man roving around the farm. Eyes glued to a chink between two boards in the barn wall, the dog watched the man stride across the field, straight toward the old fallen willow at the edge of the swampland.

107

There the man stopped, and there he stooped and searched, and once he picked up a rooster's long tail feather and dropped it again. The man had found the spot of the fearful thrashing! He came out of his stoop, and plunged straight on into the swamp. He went past the fallen willow and disappeared behind the tall brush and reeds that rimmed the swamp.

The man searched long. Even after the swamp and the fields had gone dark the beam of his flash-light flickered and ranged through the swamp. And once the dog heard him calling the little red hen, and the call sounded lost and lonely and helpless. The man's voice at once fell still, he did not call any more.

But though the swamp and the night had gone black the dog stayed, eyes glued to the chink, and still he waited. At last the beam of the flashlight came shining straight out of the swamp, and the man came past the willow again, came on across the field. He passed the barn, and went on into the house. The man was alone—he had not found the little hen.

Later the lights in the house went out, and then, at last, the dog dared plunge from the barn down into the dark wagon. He nosed a moment in the corner under the seat where the little hen always slept with him—even though he knew the little hen couldn't be there—but then he jumped down from the wagon and ran toward the spot of the fearful thrashing.

What the man had been unable to find, the dog's expert nose sniffed out in moments. He immediately snuffled out the short, zigzag trail of the little hen as she had worked and worried the egg toward the hidden nest under the tree. He did not merely smell the little hen's trail, he smelled the rolling trail of the egg. His egg—for he even smelled that it was the egg he had carried in his mouth.

It was a matter of seconds to find the little hen in the nest under the hanging tree. The big dog's tail wagged mightily. In his relief at finding the little hen he eagerly poked his nose into the nest to nuzzle her. For his trouble he got a swift, hard rap on the nose. After that one warning peck, the little hen immediately ducked back into the nest—sat dark and secret and still.

The dog waited. At last he understood that the little hen didn't intend to go to the wagon to

sleep in her every-night spot, that she intended to stay in the nest all night. It puzzled him, but he finally wormed under the leaning tree trunk the best he could, and looped his big body around the nest to spend the night protecting and guarding the little hen.

In the early dawn of Sunday morning the dog got up. He poked his nose out of the overhanging branches and leaves of the willow tree. He immediately turned back to the nest as if to tell the little hen that morning and daylight had come to the farm and that he must go into hiding, and she must go to wait for the man at the kitchen door. But the little hen sat perfectly still, didn't show the slightest intention of running to the house as she did all other mornings.

The dog became nervous. He poked his nose toward the nest again. Still the little hen didn't make the slightest move to come up out of the nest. He stood before her almost quivering with anxiety and the need to go into hiding; trembling with a hungry impatience to see if the imprisoned hen in the barn had laid an egg for him. He suddenly nudged the little hen right up out of the nest. Then under her he saw the two eggs. He rammed the little hen out of his way with his head, reached into the nest, and pulled out the one egg—*his* egg.

Fury descended on his head in the nest. The little hen was a red ball of fury, every puffed-out feather quivering with rage, head swollen with hate and rage. She came right down on the dog's head, and her wings shivered as she rained vicious pecks on his soft nose.

Even with the egg in his mouth the big dog

111

yelped out in surprise. He crawled back before her, but she didn't relent one moment, and he didn't defend himself. He backed away confused and meek—somehow knowing he had done a terrible wrong.

At last, in his confusion, he just opened his mouth and let the egg roll. Immediately the little hen's attack stopped, and she became all concern for the egg. Completely ignoring the dog, she began working the egg back to the nest. The dog lay watching and puzzling.

He lay guilty and humble, but he was not entirely unhappy. The tip of his tail even began to tremble a little as a glimmer of understanding crept into his mind. Then, as the little hen got up to turn the two eggs in the nest, he saw his egg again. The egg had been his. But the little hen had made his egg her egg. And that made her his boss. And then when he'd tried to take his egg out of the nest she had punished him for wrongdoing. That had made her his boss completely. The dog's tail twitched toward understanding.

The little hen, by punishing him, had made everything different. And much better! Now the little hen did not belong to him merely to guard and protect—she was his boss, he belonged to her. He belonged to someone! The dog swiped a big paw over his sore, pecked nose, and felt good. And he loved the little hen.

But in the nest the little hen had laid an egg. And now she came up out of the nest, paced before the dog, and cackled her triumph until it shrilled over the quiet Sunday morning fields—she the proud mother of a newly laid egg. But she settled back on the three eggs and became as silent and secret as she had been before.

Wide-eyed and pondering, the dog looked at the quiet little hen, and somehow he came to understand that she was guarding the eggs, and would not leave the nest, and that even he wasn't to be near. But then—if his little boss didn't want him here—it made him free to run to the barn to go look for an egg, and to go into hiding. He got up, wagged his tail in all respectful friendliness for the little hen, and gravely turned and ran toward the barn.

In his new happiness his tail went on wagging in friendliness at everything and nothing in the empty morning field. But when he ran into the barn, a chicken rose up in alarm under the hay loader. And as she rose the dog saw a chalky white egg under her. He immediately poked his nose toward the egg. But this chicken, too, stood her ground and struck out at him. And the dog pulled his head back, looked through the wide doorway at the distant willow tree, and wagged his tail.

The white hen also pecking him had made it sure. Whole eggs were not for him. Now he knew it surely, and he fitted it together with the other things he had learned, for he knew he was doing what his boss wanted. The little hen was his boss, and whole eggs were not for him, but belonged to his boss.

Then broken eggs were for him! He turned away and hurried up the hay loader, for up above in the hay barn was a chicken who laid broken, splattered eggs. He had never been punished for eating the broken eggs—so broken eggs were for him, whole eggs belonged to his little boss. He rammed the trap door open to look for a broken egg.

There was no egg for him in the upper barn. The white hen was fitting herself a nest in the loose hay near the big barn doors. She was making the contented little singsong sounds that meant the coming of an egg. In the middle of the barn the dog sat down on his haunches and waited hopefully for her to lay a broken egg for him.

CHAPTER VIII

The Host of Dragonflies

IT WAS ONLY minutes after the dog had crossed
the open field to hide in the barn that the man
threw open the kitchen door. The man had
overslept.

He somberly looked at the sky. "Going to
rain," he muttered. He looked at the empty doorsill before his feet. Late as it was the little hen
was not waiting for him at the kitchen door. "So
now it's sure you're dead," the man said almost
angrily toward the empty doorsill and the little
hen who wasn't there. "As I knew last night, of

116

course. But I suppose I was still hoping against hope that I'd somehow missed you in the swamp, and that you'd be sitting here again this morning."

He looked into the threatening sky again. "I'm going to enjoy eating that rooster today—if I can enjoy anything today," he told himself softly. "But I'd enjoy even more wading right into that swamp again to get my hands on whatever it was that came out of the swamp and finished off my little hen." He kicked the empty doorsill.

"But what?" he asked himself helplessly. "It was still daylight. What wild thing would come out of the swamp in daylight, chase a rooster clear to the house, and then go back and carry off the little hen?" He shook his head. "A hawk might have picked up the little hen in daylight, but I was under the hawk tree across the swamp, and there was no sign of red feathers under the hawks' nest. A dog might do something like that in daylight," he pondered.

Suddenly he threw his head up, stared straight at the barn. "The big dog!" he exclaimed. "Did he come back?" The thought startled him. "Where could he possibly keep himself?"

"Only two possible places on this little farm," he answered himself. "Up in the hay barn, or in the swamp."

He started running to the big hay doors of the barn. But he stopped before the big doors, shook his head. "He'd have to pull the bottom of one of those heavy doors out from the wall, and then squeeze through. He couldn't do it!"

Then through the thick doors he heard a slight sound inside the barn. He stepped to the latch, noiselessly undid it, and with both hands sent both doors flying out along their rusty tracks.

Right before his feet in the open doorway the startled white hen whirled up in a thunder of wings and scared cackling to the high crossbeam near the roof.

"Oh, you," the man said, disappointed. "Hey, I forgot you were still locked in here." He ran his eyes over the flat hay on the floor. Only in one corner did the hay rise in a small pile. He shook his head. "Hah, now what made me think he could be in here, when it was impossible for him to get in here in the first place?"

He looked up at the hen peering down at him over the edge of the beam. "I don't suppose you'll come down soon after the scare I gave you, so I'll just leave the doors open and you can go back to the flock in your own sweet time. Meanwhile, I've got to get to that swamp. Now that I've got that dog on the brain, I've got to satisfy myself that he isn't back. If he's back, then he killed my little red hen, and I'm going to kill him!" He turned, and almost ran to the swamp.

In the barn, long after the man was gone, the dog slowly emerged from the pile of hay in the corner. He eyed the open doors; he was troubled. The doors were wide open, but he was trapped just the same; as long as the man was around he was trapped. He turned and started to look for the man through one of the chinks between the boards in the wall. The man was striding far across the open field, straight toward the old fallen willow at the edge of the swamp. But the man went right past the willow and the little hen, plunged on into the swamp. The dog stayed at the chink.

Later it began to rain. The hard rain forced the man from the swamp, and again the dog watched in puzzlement as the man once more walked by the fallen willow tree, but came on alone. The little red hen wasn't bobbing on his shoulder.

The man came on fast as it started to rain still harder. In a pouring rain he came running past the barn. But the wide-open hay doors caught his attention. He shoved one door shut, then looked into the barn for the white hen. He did not see her on the high beam, and thinking she had gone back to the flock, he hastily shoved the other door shut, and ran on to the house.

The big doors were shut. The man was gone. The dog emerged from his hiding place under the hay once more. He immediately turned back to his spot at the chink in the end wall. It was as if it troubled him that the man had come back from the fallen willow without the little hen. The dog could not know that in her hidden nest that was for the gathering of secret eggs, the little red hen would be the most secret with the egg-gathering man. She had had to let him walk by.

The big doors remained closed. The rain clattered monotonously on the roof. But a wind swept up from the swamp and hurled rain against the

end wall of the barn. The white hen left her
nest that she had hastily fashioned again at the
doors and hurried over to the wall, began pecking at the raindrops that rolled down along the
edges of the long boards. Drop by slow rolling
drop she drank her fill.

Sometime in the afternoon the man came out
of the house in a raincoat, stood in the rain looking at the white hens wandering about the barnyard in wet misery. The dog watched the man.

"Whyn't you get some sense in your silly heads,

and get out of the rain?" the man suddenly barked at the dripping hens. "Don't be like me. What's the good of getting all soaked? No, don't be like me—wading around in a swamp in the rain looking for a dog who couldn't possibly have the brains to find his way back here." The hens poked about, did not even look up. The man shrugged his shoulders and hurried across the barnyard. He disappeared from the dog's sight in the basement of the barn.

A few moments after the man had gone into the basement the whole barn suddenly shivered and shook as from under the hay-covered floor there came the sound of a heavy, crashing blow. The dog stood rigid, but the white hen rose up from her nest, and stalked through the deep hay. Again a blow rocked the barn, shivered the hay. The chicken ran faster, her head twisting nervously, and then she bolted up to the high beam.

Under the floor, after many blows, there was a thud as a huge field stone broke from the basement wall. The dog watched the stone roll into the barnyard as its fall sent a dull, almost soundless, underground shaking through the barn. The chicken on the beam ducked out of sight. The pounding of the heavy sledge-hammer blows began again, but somehow the dog understood that it was the man breaking the big field stones out of the basement wall.

At last the pounding ended and did not resume again. The dog stood alert, ears up. The sudden silence, the completeness of the silence made the chicken nervous. She uttered a short cackle. And then an egg came rolling over the edge of the beam. It thudded, it splattered. The dog leaped toward the broken egg.

The egg devoured, the sweet, smooth feel of the egg yolk still clinging to his tongue, the dog again remembered duty and padded to the wall to search out the man and his doings. Chickens were streaming down the wet ramp—the rain had stopped. Then the dog heard the old car rattle away down the road. It was Sunday afternoon milking time on the big farm.

The dog waited for the last sounds of the car to disappear, then he lunged at the loose board and made the plunge to the wagon. He leaped down from the wagon, and started across the field. Suddenly he seemed to remember something, turned and raced to the basement of the barn.

A white egg lay under the hay loader, only partly covered with hay. The chicken was gone. Greedily the dog poked his nose into the narrow space, blundered his nose into the sharp end of a stiff, dry hay stalk. It hurt. The dog swiped a hasty paw at his nose, and remembered—whole eggs were not for him, whole eggs belonged to his boss, the little red hen.

His tail quivered, he was so pleased that he had remembered. Carefully, so as not to poke his nose into any more hay stalks, he lifted the egg with his mouth and set out to take it to his little red hen.

The dog pushed his head under the leaning trunk of the willow. His tail wagged his friendliness, he was so pleased with himself that he had thought to bring her the egg. He poked his head toward the nest to deliver the egg. The little red hen angrily lashed out at him.

The dog pulled back in confusion, hastily opened his mouth, and let the egg roll.

The little hen saw the egg. Like a ball of puffed-feather fury she came up out of the nest. She leaped at the dog, beat at him with the bony edge of her wings, drove him back from the egg.

But the moment she had him away from the egg, she ignored him. Clucking drearily, fussy and nervous, she worked the egg into her nest.

The dog looked at her in humble confusion. He was baffled, but still in a way meekly grateful that the little hen had accepted his egg. But otherwise the little hen had changed completely in the long, rainy day. She even looked different. All her feathers stuck out. She looked like a red-feather puffball. And the feather ball clucked. Clucked and clucked, drearily, endlessly. Now she settled herself on the four eggs, but the clucking went on.

The dog did not know that in the long, rainy day the little hen had become broody. The possession of eggs had brought on the broodiness, had hurried it, but broodiness would have come anyhow. It was spring—the time for being a mother. A strong instinct in the little hen had changed her in one rainy day. She had become a tyrant. She had become mean, short-tempered, and irritable—patient and tender only with the eggs. But if she had become a mean little tyrant, she could not help herself—the eggs under her were the tyrant. The eggs possessed her.

For a while the dog lay miserable on the wet ground. He became restless—he had been cooped in the barn all day. He listened to the dreary, endless cluckings. Suddenly he heaved himself up and ran from under the willow and into the swamp.

The dog splashed at the edge of the swamp, playing at catching swimming, squirming things, but his heart was not in it, and he stayed alert to the tiny soft cluckings that came to him even in the swamp. He ran splashily along the edge of the swamp, chasing nothing, and not amusing himself very much. The evening sun came out, shone flatly over the long swamp. The swamp lay in warm, misty stillness. Only the dog was noisy in a foolish, lonely water game at the edge of the swamp.

Out in the swamp a sudden evening breeze ruffled the water, and coming out of foolishness, the dog stood looking at it. But a rustling, silky whispering came to his ears—like the rustling of silk against paper. The dog stiffened. It was all about him, whispering, rustling up out of the moistness and stillness. The wind sprang up over the swamp, ruffled the dog's neck hairs. The dog's hackles rose, his lips curled back. Then it rose all around him—up from the moist and the grass and the reeds, up from the water and everywhere in the slightest whisperings of thousands on thousands of silken wings. The dog was standing in the midst of a tremendous hatch of dragonflies.

The dragonflies rose around him, then rose above him—a strange, dense cloud of insects with the sun on their wings. The hatch lifted on the wind, sifted away toward the fringe of the swampland.

And the dog, tail hanging limp, ran out before it to guard the little red hen from this strangeness. The wind died as the dog pushed under the willow tree. In a moment willow, dog, and hen were covered with dragonflies. The insects settled over everything. They covered the dog, and his skin and his hair ends shivered. But the little hen snapped at a dragonfly, she pushed out of the nest after more dragonflies. She dashed everywhere, gobbling and gobbling dragonflies. But a mass of dragonflies settled on the precious eggs, and the little hen rushed back to the nest, attacked the creeping, crawling things in a frenzy.

A wind stirred out from the swamp and the dragonfly mass lifted again, pushed across the field. Mystified, puzzled, entranced, the dog watched the drum-tight mass sift away toward the barn and the hen house.

The wind funneled the dragonflies into the space between the high barn and the hen house, and there the wind died, and there the cloud stood still. The dog ran after it, tail hanging limp in his wonderment.

In the barnyard, the white hens hurried up the long ramp, mistaking insect darkness for the coming of night. They hurried to their sleep on the roost.

But the dragonflies settled. Dragonflies blundered and massed against the walls of the hen house, slid down the walls and over the windows. The sun shone through their transparent wings on the windows, ending the brief night of the chickens. The chickens pelted down from their roost.

The first chicken poked her head out of the opening at the top of the ramp, gobbled the first crawling insect before her. She darted out of the opening to reach for the second dragonfly— the slaughter had begun. Behind the first hen the flock poured out of the hen house, pecked up dragonflies, snatched them out of the air, circled, dashed everywhere in a gorging greediness.

Then an evening breeze came over the field, channeled itself through the deep barnyard, and as the strange cloud had come, it left. It rose higher than the barn, it sifted over the house and away toward the fields across the road. The gorged chickens stood looking stupidly at each other, their crops packed and lopsided and heavy. They were drugged with dragonflies. They listlessly moved toward the ramp, silently climbed the long ramp, and though the evening sun still shone, went to their roost.

Alone the dog trudged over to the front of the house, stood staring out across the fields where the strange, tight cloud sifted into the distance. A lone cloud drifting away over fields to somewhere and nowhere, wherever the wind and their new wings would lead the dragonflies. A strange darkness, a strange loneliness sliding away in a blue, sunlit evening sky.

CHAPTER IX

Broken Eggs

IT WAS Saturday. A few bedraggled dragonflies still dangled in the cobwebs under the eaves of the barns and the house. It was the only sign left of the flight of dragonflies that six days ago had gone over the farm as briefly and mysteriously as it had come.

It was morning. The old car started rattling in the driveway of the house. The dog poked his head from under the leaves of the tipped-down branch of the willow, where he now spent his nights with the little red hen, and stood watching and listening. Behind him the little hen's cluck-ings ran on drearily. Across the field the dog saw the white heads of the flock bobbing and dip-ping as the hens hurried to scrounge up the last of the grain that the man had scattered in the barnyard. But the dog seemed in no hurry to join the flock.

At last, when all sounds of the car were gone, the dog crossed the field to the barnyard. As if from habit, he began to hunt out a few kernels of grain, but his mind did not seem to be on it—he seemed to be waiting. Once he looked up at the high barn where the white hen was still im-prisoned, but he made no effort to climb to the hay barn to see if there was a broken egg for him. He waited again.

Then it began to happen as it had happened these last three days—what the dog had been waiting for. At the top of the ramp a hen laid a shell-less egg. The egg immediately began a slow, squashy wobbling crawl down the ramp. The chicken whipped around, watched the roll-ing egg, and began chasing it down the ramp. She caught up with her egg, and gave it a hard, inquisitive peck. The peck punctured the membrane around the shell-less egg. Egg white and egg yolk dripped down from the edge of the ramp. The hen began greedily drinking at her own egg.

This was the moment for which the dog had waited. He raced across the barnyard, but at the same time there was a wild rush of all the chickens in the barnyard to the yellow egg puddle on the ground. Surrounded by pecking chickens, the dog lapped at the egg. When it was gone, he reared up, put his paws against the side of the ramp, and tried to lap up a small yellow splotch of egg yolk. A chicken whipped past his face, seized the empty membrane still lying on the ramp, and flew down with it. There was a mad chase of the chicken by the whole flock. Pieces of the dangling membrane were ripped from her beak. Now other hens ran with the pieces, and were chased in turn. The dog stood quietly in the midst of the scrambling. He waited.

Then in the middle of the barnyard two other shell-less eggs were laid, but in the mad rush for the pieces of membrane the flock paid no attention to the whole eggs. The dog quietly trotted up to the first egg, looked up at the barn, and, while looking up, stepped on the egg. He looked down, as if in surprise, to see warm egg yolk spurting from under his paw. But since the egg now was broken, and since broken eggs were his, he was free to eat the egg. He ate it.

Three mornings ago the dog had discovered it by accident. As he had crossed the barnyard he had accidentally stepped on a shell-less egg and broken it. Now, with a sort of innocent cunning, he always first looked away, then accidentally stepped on all shell-less eggs, for broken eggs were his. And by this simple, half-innocent strategy, for three days now the big dog had fed well.

The dog did not know it—nor did the hens— but it had all come about because of the great hatch of dragonflies six days before. It had resulted from the fact that the chickens had gorged themselves on dragonflies. It had been too rich a diet. Now the eggs in their egg ducts were forming too fast. There wasn't time for the last process —the forming of the hard white shell around the egg—before the eggs were laid. There was seldom time for the chickens to get to the nests. The soft, shell-less eggs took them by surprise.

Among the scurry of chickens still chasing each

other for shreds of membrane, the dog, tail wagging, trudged to the last shell-less egg that still needed stepping on—and stepped on it. Now satisfied, the dog thought of his duties toward the little red hen. He turned and loped across the field toward the willow tree.

Pleased with himself and his fullness, he poked his head through the leaves of the willow, wagged his tail for the little hen. Then, dull with his unusual fullness, he laid himself down with only his head under the tree, and promptly fell asleep.

When the dog awoke it was early afternoon, but he awoke to the same dreary, endless monotony of cluckings to which he'd fallen asleep. Beyond the tree the sky was dark, the sky threatened rain. The little hen clucked in the darkness under the tree; the dog stared at her, sleepy and bored. Then, suddenly, he heaved himself up and trotted away to play his hunting game in the swamp.

This time it was a much better game to splash around and try to catch little fish and wriggling watery things when they didn't matter as food. It was a good game to play alone. Above the swamp, against dark, hanging clouds, a hawk screamed at the dog's splashy intrusion. The dog looked up at the low-flying hawk, wagged his tail, as if pleased to have company, and deliberately splashed on again.

But rain suddenly clattered into the water, roiled the whole swamp, pelted down on the dog. The dog hurriedly left the swamp. He poked his head under the willow, but the little hen began a disturbed clucking, and the dog immediately turned and ran on across the field. The cluckings of the little hen seemed to run along after him.

The sudden hard rain had driven the chickens into the hen house. The dog peered up at the ramp. A shell-less egg lay in the opening to the hen house at the top of the ramp.

Eyeing the egg, the dog tested the ramp. He climbed carefully. He pulled himself up toward the egg by his forepaws, fitted his hind paws against the crosspieces to keep himself from sliding back. It went well until he reached the middle of the ramp, then his weight bent the plank like a hammock. His slightest move made it whipsaw and rock. The dog tried to back down; the board jogged violently. The rocking of the board released the little slide door in the wall of the

hen house; it fell shut, trapping the chickens inside. The dog slithered to the ground backward. He looked up where the egg had been, where it still must be behind the little slide door, and suddenly he ran into the horse barn and up the stairs to the high-loft hen house.

At the top of the stairs the big dog reared up and put his weight against the door. The latch released so silently, so suddenly, that the dog fell forward into the hen house. The surprised flock panicked, hurtled against the walls and the ceiling. In all the racket the dog did not see the door swing shut behind him, did not hear the slight click of the latch. At last the chickens recognized the dog and came out of panic, but they still stood with craned, wary necks in a packed group in a far corner.

The dog started toward the shell-less egg at the little slide door. He looked away, looked at the rising tier of nests, as he stepped on the egg and squashed it. With a rush the wary huddle of chickens pelted out of the corner. The dog let them struggle for the egg membrane. He smelled other eggs. He hurried to the tier of nests.

He poked his nose into a nest in the lowest tier. A broken shell-less egg lay among a few with white shells. He licked up what was left of the broken egg, carefully licked off the yolk-messed shells of the other eggs. He went to the next nest. Three chickens in a higher tier broke from their nest. Interested, the dog reared up, placed his paws on the perch before the high nests, and saw an unbroken shell-less egg. But he could not step on an egg in a high nest. It posed a problem. He considered it. His tail waved vaguely, thought-fully. It was a problem.

On the big farm the hard, sudden rain had driven the farmer and Joe, the hired man, into the barn. The two squatted on their haunches just inside the doorway, and watched the relentless fall of the rain.

"Looks like nothing but rain the rest of the day, Joe," the farmer said. "If you ask me it's a good day for sleeping in the hay, and you look as if you could stand an afternoon in the hay."

"Oh, I don't need sleep," Joe said casually. "Anyway, I wouldn't sleep. All I've got on my mind is the remodeling of that barn." He stared into the rain. Suddenly he gave his knee a hard slap.

"What was that for?" the farmer demanded.

"Well, I'm puzzled. Monday and Tuesday I still had a full lay—sixty-five and seventy eggs. And that's right for this time of the year. It's spring—every hen should be laying. But ever since Wednesday the flock's been going down steadily. And last night I collected only thirteen eggs."

"Hunh, that's strange. But how's that remodeling coming?" the boss said.

Joe shrugged. "About the speed it would go

when you don't have time, don't have money, and just have old horse-stable lumber to work with. I even smell like a horse just from working with that lumber."

The farmer grinned.

"Just thirteen eggs from that whole flock," Joe said morosely. "And I'd figured on using that egg money for some new lumber. I can't make it all from old horse stables. Besides, I need wiring and electrical equipment. . . . Wire the barns for light," he joked, "then I could work all night long." He looked almost wistfully up at the high haymow. "Sleep!" he said shortly. "I've got problems! As if worrying about money and lumber and wiring isn't enough, something's going on there at my place—the rooster's driven to his death, the little hen disappears, and now no eggs."

The boss looked interested. "You mean you kept that toeless runt that you were suffering over a while back, and that I told you to kill and eat? Joe, farming is business! Fussing with toeless chickens is not business. I know you hope to build that place into a poultry farm, but you'll never do it by petting around with a two-cent hen."

"No, I guess not," Joe muttered. Suddenly he flared, looked straight at the farmer. "Could you have killed and eaten that mare—supposing you liked horse meat—if something had happened to her that night the colt was coming?"

The farmer winced. "You're talking about a three-thousand-dollar mare—not a chicken."

"A five-thousand-dollar mare or a two-cent chicken," Joe said hotly, "what's the difference? And if I didn't fuss and pet and try to understand a two-cent hen, what do you think I'd have been worth that night with the mare and the colt when you were chewing your fingernails down to the knuckles?"

The farmer got a queer look on his face. "Joe," he said evenly, "I see you know that I sold that mare and colt for a cool five thousand dollars, and not for three thousand. But don't think I'm not grateful. Oh, I know I've been letting it slide, I know I'm tight, but I'd honestly planned to reward you for saving that mare." He glanced up at the haymow, struggled in his mind with himself. "All right, I'll go up in the hay and do your sleeping for you. But you get yourself to town—order what you need to wire that barn for light, and have them send the bills to me."

A startled Joe rose to his feet, speechless.

The farmer held up his hand as if to silence the

speechless Joe. "Gwan, run to the old car and get going," he said roughly. "I'll get up in that haymow and start examining my head—must be something wrong with it when I help the best hired man I ever had to start a poultry farm of his own."

He climbed heavily. But when he looked down, Joe was still there, staring up at him. "Hey, get going," the farmer said. "You make me uncomfortable. I'm not much for good deeds, and I'd better quick sleep it off. Be back for the milking, hunh?"

Joe wasn't listening. He started for the car, turned and came running back. "The first thing is to wire the basement and the barnyard for light, then I can work on for hours after dark," he shouted up to the farmer. He pounded away through the rain without waiting for an answer.

The car stopped in the driveway beside the house. The man hurried through the rain to the kitchen door, but stopped. "Better chase the chickens in out of the wet and mud," he muttered, and turned and ran to the barnyard.

There wasn't a chicken in the barnyard. At the top of the ramp the slide door was shut. The man threw a startled glance at it. "Somebody closed the little door and locked up the hens." He charged up the stairs.

The flock heard him pounding up the stairway and came crowding to the door. Beyond the packed flock, in the middle of the hen house, stood the dog. The man stared at the dog. Then the dog's courage oozed away. He lay down flat before the man—meek, guilty, hopeless.

"About the happiest day of my life," the man said slowly. "And there you are! And you've been here all the time! That's where the eggs and the little hen went. Killed the rooster, ate the little hen, and now it's eggs." His arms hung heavy and straight beside him. He plowed through the flock, came at the dog, hands hanging. "With my bare hands," he muttered. "Egg yolk still on your nose. Killed the little hen. . . . With my own hands," he softly repeated, as if in a daze.

But his eyes shifted to the tier of nests. The yolk of an egg dripped from a high nest. It momentarily distracted the man. Suddenly he turned to the nest, peered into it, looked at the front edges of other nests stained with egg yolk. "Rolled them out, didn't you? Broke them against the edge of the nests. But why you took them out of the high nests, when there's all kinds of eggs in the lower nests in easy reach—" He pulled a white egg out of a nest, examined it. "You spilled yolk all over the shell of this egg, and then you licked it clean. But you didn't take it and eat it. Why?"

Suddenly he looked from the egg to his hand. He grimaced. "With my bare hands! I was going to choke you with my hands—and I could have right then! But it's all lost in talk again." He shoved the egg into the nest. "I got to get cleaned up, get to town before I waste everything in talk. Come along."

The straw on the floor pushed up before the dog as he crawled his humble, obedient way after the man. At the top of the stairs the man held the door open. He had to pass the man. But the man in his haste squeezed the door shut on the dog's tail. The dog yelped a small miserable yelp that he hastily swallowed. Behind the man he oozed silently down the stairs.

But instead of hurrying to the house to clean up, the man darted across the yard to the basement of the barn, stood in the doorway in a sudden excited estimating of all he was going to need to bring electricity to the barn. His mind busy, he quite forgot the dog was lying in meek flatness behind him, and stepped over the dog as he backed away from the barn. The man walked backward all the way from the barn to the house, eyeing and estimating the distance. The dog crept along before the backing man.

His mind still on his figures, the man threw open the kitchen door, but then stood preoccupied again. He mumbled and calculated. The confused dog lay before the sill of the open door not knowing what was expected of him. Then, when the man continued standing and mumbling, he miserably crawled past the man's feet into the house, and crept under the kitchen table.

In a few moments the man came hurrying into the kitchen, began tugging at his clothes. He rubbed a nervous hand over his chin. "Got to shave. . . . Let's see now, how many insulators should it take? A thousand feet of wiring should do it—just so I've got good light in the basement, and a big spotlight for the barnyard. . . . Switches. . . . Golly, what a mindful of things."

He began shaving, began humming as he shaved. "You know," he said into the mirror as he scraped with a long, straight razor, "you act meek and boneless and brainless, but you must be smart as a whip—sneaking in here while you figured my mind was busy with other things, thinking maybe in that way you could get yourself a home."

His razor stopped dead on his cheek. He whipped around, hunched down, and peered under the table. "Now how'd you get in here so quick? My head's buzzing with figures, but with some part of my mind I must have known you were under the table—I was talking to you. . . . Yeah, you're smart as a whip, and smart as you are you'd be something to talk to—in a way, I suppose, almost as good as the little red hen. . . ."

The dog lay flat, head stretched between his paws, eyes staring straight ahead over the floor, but at the new tone in the man's voice his tail suddenly gave the table leg a hard slap. Then he lay still again.

The man hunched beside him, looked him over curiously. For a moment he touched the drying soap on his face, then he thoughtfully fingered the sharp razor. "You know," he said slowly, "I could have killed you that first moment in the hen house, but I talked again, talked myself out of it. . . . But hanged if I talk myself into keeping you. I could forgive your stealing eggs and killing the rooster, but there's one thing remains —if you came back, if you were here all these days, then you killed my little red hen, and that's something I can't forgive, and won't talk myself out of. I can't kill you now any more, but I *can* lose you right in the middle of the busy business section of the town." He got up. "Come along. I'm going to lose you in that town, but right now I'm going to lock you in the car while I get ready, otherwise I might talk myself into keeping you— just by talking to you. Come along."

Face covered with dried lather, bare shoulders quivering to the cold rain, the man walked to the car and yanked the door open. The dog in silent hopelessness flowed up to the seat. The man slammed the door shut.

CHAPTER X

The Journey Home

FOR LONGER than two weeks the big dog had been gone from the farm. A country dog, he had evidently not been able to find his way out of the confusion of buildings and traffic and streets of the business section in the heart of the big town. This time, it seemed, the man had thoroughly lost him when he'd suddenly shoved him out of the car as a traffic light changed, and had gone roaring around a corner in the heavy, confusing traffic.

For over two weeks the big dog had been gone

from the little hen in the secret nest under the willow tree. He had run across the field that long ago day of the sudden, hard rain, and he had not come back to her, not even in the long, dark, dangerous nights at the edge of the swamp. And this was the third week of the little red hen in the hidden nest under the tipped-down willow —the end of her third week of brooding out the five eggs in the nest. It was a morning of one of the endless days and nights of the third week.

The little hen on the nest was but a bundle of skin and bones and broken, worn, untidy feathers. She was weak and starved. She now left the nest only to drink at a nearby, swampy hole just outside the hanging branches of the willow. Water she had to have; food she had to do without, because of her fear of the hawks.

Once—oh, it seemed long ago—there had been the dragonflies. The rich, lush diet of dragonflies the little hen had gorged on then had produced the fifth and last egg to add to the marvelous hoard in the secret nest. But the rainy day that the man had taken the dog away and lost him in town, the hard rain had dissolved the last dragonflies.

And now with the protection of the dog gone, with her food gone, and because of the hawks, the little red hen was in a race—a slow, dragged-out three weeks' race between starving to death and brooding five chicks out of the five eggs.

But across the swamp, tall in the top of a naked, dead tree, rose the mass of untidy twigs that was the nest of the hawks. In that nest—also brooding on eggs—sat the mother hawk The male hawk, bold, driven, made fearless by the two eggs and the brooding mother hawk in the nest, no longer confined himself in his hunting to the far reaches of the swamp. Daily now he patrolled the field as far as the barnyard. He kept the little hen from hurriedly running across the field to the flock to pick up the grain that the man scattered over the barnyard before going to work.

The real danger, the real enemy, however, was the female hawk, who, like the little hen, was also trying to become a mother. Over the rim of the big nest high in the tree she surveyed the whole swamp. Her keen, sharp eyes always caught the first movements of the little starved hen whenever she tried to emerge from under the dense willow to strip seeds from the swamp weeds and grasses for just a little food. The mother hawk was also hungry and starved—often the male hawk failed in the hunt. At sight of the little hen, the hawk, bold, driven by hunger and the need quickly to get back to the cooling eggs in her nest, would sweep out over the swamp toward the willow tree, and the little starved hen would have to scuttle back under its dense cover. Then for long moments the hawk would hang over the tree. Her bold, eerie, reckless screaming would fall down on the little hen, would curdle her blood, would freeze the little hen down on the eggs in the nest. There were times when the hawk actually landed in the tip of the tree, and the branches would sway and the leaves would rustle as the little hen cowered in the nest under the leaning trunk. The hungry mother hawk was starving the little red mother hen to death by confining her to the willow tree.

Strangely, the hawks made the days at the edge of the dangerous swamp much more fearful than the long, dark nights. But that was because of the dog. Though the little hen did not know it, and the dog, lost in the town, could not know it, he was still protecting his little hen in the nights.

The scent of the big dog was still trapped under the tight willow tree. The hanging branches and leaves had enclosed the dog's scent. The little hen gave off almost no scent in her broodiness. The prowling wild animals of the night caught the stronger scent of the dog long before the scent of the little hen could reach their keen, hunting noses. They crashed away from the dog scent, hurried back into the swamp for their hunting.

In a way, too, the man was helping the little hen through the nights, even though he did not know it any more than did the dog he had banished to the town. The man had wired the barn and the barnyard for light. Now he worked long hours every night to remodel the basement into a hen house. His hammering and his pounding, and the bright light shining from the barnyard and raying across the flat field almost to the willow tree, kept most of the wild animals to the back reaches of the big swamp. The man, too, was helping his little red hen, at least in the early hours of the night.

But this was the day—perhaps the last day of the little hen's long brooding—and the danger of the hawks came back with the morning. In the early dusk, while she was still invisible to the hawks, the little hen had hurriedly drunk at the stale muddy pothole just outside the willow tree, then she had scuttled back to the nest. Now the morning wore on, but a wind sprang up over the swamp. The wind and the threatening clouds racing low over the swamp promised nothing but a raw, cold, wet day. Suddenly a hawk screamed right above the tipped-down willow tree, and the little hen cowered in the nest.

The wind brought the scream of the hawk to the dog. The wind brought to his nostrils the smell of the swamp. On the high hill where he stood, the dog's bedraggled tail wagged, and he started forward again. But there were other hills, many fields, many hills, before he staggered down to the swamp's flatness. He stumbled into the back reaches of the swamp under the naked tree of the hawks.

The mother hawk peered in wrathful silence over the edge of the nest down at the dog. But the male hawk, riding under windy wisps of clouds over the swamp, came down from the sky in a whistling dive. His wings screeched, and his talons raked air inches above the dog. The hawk climbed back to the clouds for courage for a new attack on the dog, and the wind took his wrathful scream and stretched it across the sky. But the exhausted dog under the tree paid the hawk no attention, hardly lifted his head as the thin wing sounds whistled close above him again. At last he bestirred himself and pushed on along the edge of the swamp toward home.

The dog shoved his nose under the rustling, tossing willow. The startled little hen rose up in the nest. A quiver of delight ran through the dog, his tail waved a big wag for the little hen, but he could not wait, he was too starved, he had to go home—had to find food. The little red hen silently settled back on the eggs.

In the barnyard a few wind-blown hens tacked awkwardly as the wind slammed against their broad tails and shoved them off course. But the hawk had followed the dog; the hawk screamed wrathfully in the sky. The chickens rushed up the ramp to seek safety and shelter with the rest of the flock inside the hen house.

The dog stood alone in the barnyard. The dog looked perplexed at the strange barnyard and the changes the man had brought to it and the barns. He gravely studied the yawning holes the man had made in the basement wall of the big barn. The lower horse barn had become a shell. The ramp still led to the high-loft chicken coop, but the hen house rested on the bare corner posts of the lower barn. The high hen house stood as if on stilts. All the boards had been pulled off the lower barn, only the naked posts remained. Beyond the bare posts even the horse stables inside the lower barn had been partly dismantled.

The bewildered dog trudged to the wide doorway of the basement barn. Again he stood still. The hay loader no longer rose beside the doorway. Where it had stood there was nothing but a heap of mortar dust and chipped stones. Against the back wall rose a tier of nests and a partly built roost.

The dog's tail wavered dubiously, then he hurriedly turned from the doorway and trudged to the house. The potato crate that had once held feed for the little red hen leaned upended and empty against the wall of the house. But the gate in the fence around the little parsnip garden was wide open. The dog hurried through the gate. One by one he pulled up the last remaining parsnips, and wolfed them down. A sudden rain squall drove him from the garden back to the barn.

There was no shelter in the open basement. The big dog stood mute and miserable, looking again at the new strangeness. The wind hurled through the yawning openings; rain lashed and swept over the floor. The dog looked up at the trap door, high and unreachable. Suddenly he turned and set out through the rain to the fallen willow at the edge of the swamp.

On his big meal of parsnips the dog ran almost sturdily, and his tail began to wag as he neared the tree. He crawled gratefully under the shelter of the low-hanging willow, crawled almost to the nest and the little red hen.

The little hen watched him quietly, did not lash out at him, her whole mind seemed to be on the eggs—as if she were waiting, as if she were listening to the eggs under her.

Only the little hen heard the soft click of the egg. Now the egg stirred under her, rolled a little. The little hen rose, tenting her wings over the edge of the nest, spreading them wide against the great things happening under her. Suddenly she searched under her ruffled feathers; with a careful bill she pushed, and nudged, and then with a soft, gentle wing she tucked a little yellow chick tight against her warm body.

The dog's eyes jumped wide as for a moment he saw the liveness of the chick that hadn't been there the moment before—that had been an egg. The little hen rose up again. Another egg had started wobbling, and tenderly the little hen rolled it over. A new chick stepped out of the broken halves of its egg. The little hen settled over it, and softly, securely her wings closed over two chicks.

The big dog lay rigid, motionless, eyes steadfast on the great wonder.

In the nest the little hen was raising up for a last time. Now her round knucklebones were planted among broken shells of eggs and four stirring, peeping chicks. Against one foot the last egg rocked, wobbled, and almost circled the little round knucklebone. It continued stirring, acting alive, but nothing happened. The little hen pushed her bill toward the egg, gently tapped the egg. Under her bill the egg exploded in the tiniest of explosions. The shell fell apart and a moist chick stood up, looked up, and began peeping at its new mother. The four earlier chicks cheeped and peeped along with it.

But now the little hen did not settle back on her chicks. She stood ready, wings gently lifted, tenting the chicks, but not closing down over them. The long patience and the long wait were over. Now there could be no more waiting. The journey home had to begin. The little hen stepped out of the nest, clucked a new clucking to her five chicks.

The dog heaved himself to his feet, eagerly pushed from under the willow—eager to go home with the little red hen.

Under the willow, as if the soft cluckings pulled them up one by one, the four chicks came tumbling over the rim of the nest. But the last little chick had trouble getting up the steep sides. The little hen turned and over the rim clucked the desperately cheeping chick up out of the depths of the nest. She lifted her wing and let the last chick run under it for just a moment. Then, with the soft cluckings streaming out behind her, she led the five chicks from under the tree on their long journey home. She clucked them along, forcing the chicks to follow her, finding for them the little paths among the tall grass and the taller weeds. She coaxed, directed, commanded. Her head twisted everywhere to see that they obeyed and stayed near.

The big dog walked a few steps, waited, walked again—led the way home for her and her brood. But the sweep of the wind was over the field, the wind flattened and tangled the lush, long grass of spring. The tiny chicks were engulfed in a

waving sea of grass. They struggled and muddled among grass and weeds ten times taller than they. The field was a sea and a confusing jungle, but always there was the eternal soft streamer of cluckings from their little red mother to lead them on.

A loudly cheeping chick suddenly got itself completely lost in the towering forest of stalks that was a weed clump. It was dark under the weeds, and the chick all at once fell silent. Suddenly all the peeping chicks were silent. Somehow the four chicks had found the fifth under the sheltering dark leaves, and since it was dark the five huddled in silence in the darkness. The little hen became frantic.

The dog came running back. The dog easily nosed out the chicks under the weeds. He stood over the group as the little hen gathered her brood, clucking her relief, clucking her love.

High above the field the male hawk let himself be swept along under the scudding clouds. In a moment he swept far beyond the field. But brazen, bold eyes had in that moment looked down on the little group in the field. The hawk had seen the movement of five yellow chicks deep down in the wind-flattened grass. The hawk let himself be swept as far as the house. Then, clambering up to higher crosscurrents of air, he winged toward the nest in the naked tree where the mother hawk sat sheltering two newly-hatched young. From high above the swamp the male screamed a long scream across the windy sky to alert his mate in the nest.

The mother hawk swept up from the nest, let the wind take her low over the swamp and the field. Infinitely higher than she, the male sailed over the field. Then he hovered, circled above a spot in the field where a big dog stood.

The dog started to move across the field toward the faraway barns. Now the mother hawk also saw the quick, bright movement of the yellow chicks. At that moment the male started to fall down from the sky toward the chicks. But the female flew forward a few wing flaps, forced him to break his dive. He braked himself just below her, came climbing up to her. She circled him angrily, eyes down on the field, impatient with him. She forced him high into the sky, went with him, forcing the wait there for the time when the chicks would step from the wind-tangled grass to the bare ground of the barnyard.

In the struggle with the wind and waving grass

and the five bewildered chicks, the little red hen remained unaware of the high hawks. But she kept close to the dog, and she kept her chicks close.

The rain squalls had driven the men on the big farm into the barn. They sat hunched down on their heels, shivering a little in their wet clothes as wind and rain swept into the barn.

"Joe, close those doors, I'm chilled to the bone," the farmer said. "If that rain had held off an hour," he grouched, "we'd have finished seeding that rye field. Well, I guess we can stand a Saturday afternoon in the hay. Can't we, Joe?" he said softly. "Joe!" He laughed.

Joe was rocking on his heels, nodding, tipping, waking—sleeping again. He caught himself, laughed confusedly with the farmer. "The moment I sit still," he said dazedly. "I think I could sleep standing up—like a horse."

"That I can believe," the farmer said. "I was out your way yesterday—looking at the swampland. I'd been thinking of turning the cows in there, but now with this rain . . . But what I was going to say, while I was out that way, I walked over from the swamp to have a look at your barn. Man, what you've accomplished in a couple of weeks! Don't you sleep at all?"

"Four hours every night," Joe said shortly. "Four hours," he told the farmer earnestly, "is enough."

"Don't waste your time trying to convince me," the farmer said. "I can't get along on ten. But, Joe, does that barn have to be rebuilt in a week? You've got till winter, and it's still spring. "Say—" He interrupted his thoughts, "one thing. What's those rubber flippers nailed above the doorway to that basement? Is it some kind of good-luck business—instead of horseshoes—now that horses are going out of style?"

Joe grinned. "The flippers? Oh, those are still from my days of foolishness. They were for the little red hen. I hate to tell you, but I tried to fit her with rubber feet. Well, I guess I nailed them up above the door as a sort of a sign of my growing up and as a sort of memorial to the little red hen, who started all that remodeling."

The farmer sat looking puzzled, but then grinned in a sort of old-man fondness at Joe rocking sleepily on his heels again. "A funny thing, and I've been meaning to tell you," he said loudly. "You know, I visited your place way back. Oh, when was it? Some Sunday when it rained all day. Well, anyway, then, too, I went to have a look at the swamp pasture land."

His voice droned on. "Well, there I was way back of the swamp when I saw a queer cloud go up from your barns and house, but I was too far back to see what it was. Well, I never put two and two together until yesterday I happened to mention that queer cloud to my wife, and she told me there'd even been an item in the paper about it—some unusual hatch of dragonflies. But don't you see? That must have been it. Your chickens stuffed themselves on dragonflies and then they laid nothing but shell-less eggs. Remember how you fussed about it—they were down to thirteen eggs a day, and all that? But that must have been it—I forgot to tell you."

"Yeah, that must have been it," Joe said vaguely. He was nodding again. Suddenly he sat wide-eyed. "Shell-less eggs, did you say?" He stared straight ahead. "Then that is what the dog did," he mumbled to himself. "Took the eggs without shells out of the nests, but just licked off the eggs with shells, never touched them. But why?"

"Look, boy, get up in that hay," the farmer ordered. "You're mumbling in your sleep."

"No, I'm wide awake now," Joe said earnestly. "And running through the rain to the old car will wake me up some more. I can't afford to waste a windfall like this—a whole rainy afternoon to work on the new hen house." He jumped up and hurried out of the barn to give the farmer no chance to argue him out of it.

He came back. "The car won't start—the wind drove the rain up under everything."

"Take mine," the farmer said. "No, hold it. I forgot, you don't have a garage. The rain's stopped now, but that's a brand-new car, and I hate to have it standing out in all kinds of weather."

"I could—wouldn't it be all right if I put the car up in the hay barn?" Joe hastily suggested.

"Sure, that'll do it. But don't fall asleep on the way."

"In a brand-new car—fall asleep?"

The new car came smoothly sliding up the

driveway, purred on beyond the house, and stopped before the big hay doors of the barn. The man got out, opened the doors, drove the car in the barn, and then, with careful concern for the beautiful car, closed the barn doors again. From the high beam the white hen peered in secret silence down on the man and the glossy car. Her bobbing head and neck reflected themselves in the shiny top. She saw her own reflection move. She panicked and pelted in squawky flight down from the high beam, crashed against the end wall of the barn, and landed in a stunned heap at the foot of the wall.

The man looked at her in surprise, and hurried to her. "Golly, you still here?" he said in amazement. "And I thought you'd gone back to the flock that rainy day I left the doors open for you." But as he stooped to pick up the stunned hen, he happened to glance down through a chink between two of the boards of the end wall. He rose, stood rigid. The chicken stirred at his feet, but the man made soft, unbelieving sounds to himself. He pointed down to the field. "The little hen!" he whispered. Then he just stared at the little procession in the field below—the dog, the little red hen, and the five strung-out chicks. The little group was reaching the barnyard. Up in the barn the man shifted his position, hurried over to the side wall, followed the chinks, not knowing he was doing exactly what the big dog had always done in following his movements. And the dog almost straight below the man, not having been alerted by the rattletrap car, was totally unaware of the silent man. The dog stepped from the grassy field into the bare barnyard.

At the edge of the barnyard the dog stopped, turned his head almost as if he were asking the little hen where she wanted him to lead her and her chicks. But a sudden wind squall brought the dog to a hasty decision. He hustled to the wide doorway and into the basement of the barn. Behind him the little red hen now pushed from among the tall grass, hurried her cluckings to hurry the chicks. The first chick popped out of the grass, scurried over the bareness of the yard after its mother. One by one the chicks popped from the grass. Now all five chicks were running across the barnyard.

At that moment past the barn wall, past the man's startled eyes, something big, dark whistled out of the sky. The little hen heard the rush of the hawk's wings at the same moment. She spread her own wings, clucked wild warnings, swept her wings down on her chicks, swept them against her, squashed herself down over the chicks, sat bowed, frozen, waiting. . . .

Up in the barn the man raced wildly along the wall, grabbed at a wallboard, grabbed at another. Suddenly the loosened board he had grabbed yawned out from the wall, and the man looked down into the deep wagon box and the barnyard.

The female hawk rushing down to the earth, her steep dive aimed at the last little chick, saw the chick disappear under the wing at the last moment. The hawk tried to swoop up, but it was too late to snap cleanly out of her steep, headlong dive. Outstretched talons raked the little hen's wings, talons closed, scooped her up from the huddled chicks. The hawk's rushing speed lifted the little hen in the air. The hawk struggled, flapping great wings, beating them against the weight of the little hen. The talons set deeper as the hawk struggled wildly to get up from the earth among the confining, threatening closeness of the high barn walls.

A wild squawk pressed out of the little hen. The man looked helplessly from the high barn to the deep wagon box far below him. The chicks ran in confused, cheeping circles, peeping up at their mother. But the dog in the basement of the barn heard the squawk. He whirled, and hurtled himself through the nearest jagged hole in the wall. At the sailing leap of the dog the frightened hawk tried to lunge up into the sky. The dog came, vengeful mouth open, jaws wide. But the dog overleaped, his jaws snapped air, and he crashed against the struggling hawk.

Hawk and dog and chicken tumbled down to the ground together. The hawk struggled up, freed her talons, freed her wings, beat the air. Powerful wings beat in the dog's face. The hawk croaked and hissed threatening, desperate sounds. Then her wings were flapping her up. She lifted heavily, struggled her way back into the sky.

The man came running around the barn toward the little group standing shaken and bewildered in the windy barnyard. "Ah, that was splendid, splendid," he gasped out to the big dog. "You saved her, and you hadn't killed her as I thought. Why, you must have guarded her in that swamp. And you led her home! And now you're home, too, big fellow. You're home! And we've got to find a big name for you. Oh, that was splendid."

He suddenly looked up into the sky. "There she still is, and now he's joined her, and they're waiting again bold as brass. Ah, hawks are splendid. Hawks are splendid, too, big fellow." But the hawk screamed in the sky, and the little hen scuttled under the dog and opened her wings and clucked frantically, and the peeping chicks ran under her, and were silent as death under her wings.

The man looked at them. "What am I standing here talking for? Come along." He turned hastily and started toward the house. The big dog's tail wavered a question, but then he obediently followed the man. The little hen got up and hurried after the dog, and the five chicks streamed after their clucking mother. The man threw open the kitchen door.

The dog hesitated, but the door stood wide open, and the dog stepped over the sill. Behind the little hen four of the chicks tumbled over the sill, and the man grinned down at them as with tiny, click-clacking nails they skittered over the kitchen linoleum to their mother.

But a thin streamer of a cry came down the windy avenues of the sky—lost, defiant, proud, and vengeful, and the man tilted his head and looked up at the hawks. "Still waiting," he muttered. "Bold as brass, and waiting for revenge. Hawks sure are brazen, and, in a way, splendid. Splendid!"

But the last chick was having trouble getting over the doorsill. The man stooped, put a hand under it, and with a soft pat and push lifted the chick over the sill. "Come on, you little caboose that the hawk didn't get. Get in that kitchen—

the box with straw that I fixed long ago for your mother is still waiting behind the kitchen stove —and you belong to this family, too."

The chick, peeping wildly, scurried over the linoleum to its clucking mother. The man closed the kitchen door.

He closed the door behind the little hen and her five chicks, and behind the little hen's big dog.

He closed the door of the dog's new home. And that was splendid, too. Ah, that was splendid.

The big dog's tail swished wildly over the little hen and her five chicks, and the tail slapped and slapped against the leg of the kitchen table. For hadn't he known that the man was kind, and the man was good? And wasn't that also splendid?